BREATHE

BREATHE

a novel

by
Jessica Laurie

Wyatt House Publishing

Mobile, Alabama
www.wyattpublishing.com

Wyatt House books may be ordered through booksellers or by contacting:

WYATT HOUSE PUBLISHING
399 Lakeview Dr. W.
Mobile, Alabama 36695
www.wyattpublishing.com
editor@wyattpublishing.com

Because of the dynamic nature of the Internet, any web address or links contained in this book may have changed since publication and may no longer be valid.

Cover design by: Mark Wyatt

ISBN 13: 978-0-9915798-2-2

Printed in the United States of America

This book is dedicated to...

My Pappaw, who taught me the value of
family, education, work, and enjoying God
by simply living his life.

I miss you, and I love you.

Thanks.

PROLOGUE

Falling.

Cold. Sharp. Hard.

I steeled my jaw with a wince then grew still. A million pin prickles skittered up and down my skin as if my entire body was waking up after being kept in a numb slumber. Curling on my side, I squeezed my eyelids shut. I didn't want to wake up.

Not yet.

The skitter of footsteps tap danced through my skull, reverberating through my cheek pressed against the smooth, slick floor.

"Is she all right?" a frantic woman's cry hovered somewhere above me.

Stirring, my hand brushed against something hard and cool. My eyes opened.

Like trying to focus through a telescope lens, my vision blurred before zeroing into razor sharp focus on an object lying a few inches from my face.

Still struggling to gather my wits, I stroked the side of the small object with a delicate touch and drew it closer.

A key. Brass. Length of my palm. Antique-looking with the top shaped like a three-leaf clover.

As I continued to study the random object, awareness seeped into the edges of my mind and vision—it was snowing.

I bolted upright with a low gasp. How had I ended up outside?

Sitting alone in the middle of a dirt path, I was surrounded by patches of thin silver ice and snow. The crystals glimmered from snatches of sunlight filtering through the clouds and tree canopy towering high above.

I stretched my free hand towards the closest patch of ice. A reflection of my fingers appeared as they hovered close to its surface. Even though I didn't touch the frozen water I could feel the coolness stinging my palm.

"Don't move her! Wait for the paramedics," a man's voice ordered. "Where's her sister? Find her sister, now!"

The warmth of a thousand bodies pressed in around me, but a coldness had seeped into my skin that I didn't think would ever leave.

Snatching back my hand, tremors coursed through my arms and legs. The rough edges of the key teeth bit into my hand as I clenched it and pressed my fist hard against my aching forehead. If only the noise would stop. If everything would just stop.

Like a chorus of ghouls, the sound of high-pitched sirens pierced my ears.

"Clear the way!"

Clattering and murmurs.

"Hi, young lady, can you hear me?" someone asked in a low tone. "If you can hear me, I need you to respond. We need you to wake up."

A moan caught in my throat as prickles of fear pinched the back of my neck and trickled down my spine.

A heavy presence was behind me. Watching. Waiting.

Hands trembling, I slowly rose to my feet and turned around.

A hundred yards away, clouds of darkness were coiled like a beast ready to pounce. The darkness roiled with shades of gray, black, and purple like a moody thunderstorm, emitting grumbles, as though waiting impatiently for me to move so it could have the thrill of chasing its prey. To trap me.

I was frozen. Even the trembling had stopped, though it felt like ice water had replaced the blood in my veins.

A wail exploded through the woods—coming straight from the center of the darkness.

Pure panic from a deep, familiar part of myself took over my body, and I whirled around, losing my balance. Stumbling, my hands broke my fall, though I still managed to keep hold of the key. Pieces of ice, like glass, pierced my hands and bare feet, but I barely noticed.

Shoving off the ground, I broke into a dead sprint up the path. I didn't know where I was going, but I couldn't remain still.

I couldn't stay anymore.

A low roar rose from behind me, and I braved a look over my shoulder.

That was a mistake.

The darkness had grown into a giant wall that swallowed the trees on either side of the path and diminished any light that had been streaming from overhead. With a rumbling heave, it lunged forward and rushed after me. Another wail rent the air.

"She's not responding. Why isn't she responding?" a young woman's familiar voice floated around me.

"We're doing all we can. We'll know more when—"

"No! You have to do something now! Sh-she's slipping away." She began to weep.

Turmoil crashed through my being as I flew down the path with trees blurring past me and black pressing in behind me. A sob rose in my throat.

"Come back. Please come back!"

"No," I gasped. "No!"

Back? If I turned back the darkness would overcome me and

there would be nothing left.

Each breath I took sent searing pain through my side. I couldn't hold out much longer.

Looking up, I screamed, "Help me! Help—" My voice broke. "Please."

The path careened to the right, and I stumbled to a stop, nearly falling again. All I could do was stand in the middle of the dirt pathway, gasp in quick breaths, and stare.

In front of me was a stone wall. Rough sandy, gray, and caramel stones encased in creamy mortar towered higher than I could see, stretching into the heavens. Dark green ivy tangled between the stones and mortar, as though adding even more support to the impenetrable barrier.

The only way to get past the wall, it seemed, was through an arched, wooden door set into the stones. The path ran straight to the door, as if this was where it was meant to lead to all along.

Relief surged through me. I could hide in there.

Grasping the doorknob, I attempted to turn it, but it stopped fast. Locked.

"No." Groaning, I slapped my palm flat against the dense wood. "No! Let me in." As I pounded harder, the forgotten key slipped from my grasp, falling to the soft ground.

My breath stopped. A locked door. A key. No way.

The wailing of the darkness intensified, and I made a quick decision. Snatching up the key, I shoved it into the lock, and with a swift twist, the door opened. Relieved laughter tumbled from my lips.

"I'm so sorry," the young woman said softly. "So sorry."

My laughter faded, hands trembling. I hesitated, glancing over my shoulder one more time.

The darkness whipped around the bend with a scream.

A gasp choked me as I scrambled through the doorway, yanked

the key from the lock, and heaved the door shut. Jamming the key into the other side of the keyhole, I twisted hard until I heard a click indicating it was locked again. I stepped back on trembling legs, clutching the key with both hands against my chest.

Energy poured out of me like water swirling down a drain.

Brilliant colors blurred around the corners of my vision as I fell. A set of arms caught me.

"You're safe," a warm, deep voice whispered in my ear.

Safe.

The word caressed me, wrapping around me like a favorite blanket.

One more word brushed my thoughts before I completely slipped away. One word that I knew meant something but couldn't quite place.

Hope.

Wisely and slow; they stumble that run fast.
William Shakespeare, Romeo and Juliet

CHAPTER ONE

Dillon

They were American.

Great.

Dillon refrained from ducking beneath the bar of Brannigan's Pub like some little boy afraid of his own shadow. Maybe he was.

Instead, he concentrated on wiping down the already clean counter with an old bandanna as he stole glances of the two girls and one guy who'd just stumbled in the door to escape the sudden downpour.

Judging from their accents associated with their ceaseless chatter, they were definitely American. They looked around his age, nineteen, or a bit older. Probably college students studying abroad who decided to go sight-seeing around Ireland and ended up in the one-horse town of Kerryglen.

Just his luck.

Thankfully, even though he was the only one out front working the place and they were the only customers besides Old Man Cagney, who was distracted by his newspaper, they didn't seem to notice him as they made their way to a corner table.

As they settled into their seats, Dillon took the opportunity to duck into the kitchen where the pub owner and head cook, Colin Brannigan, was adjusting the antenna on his ancient television. The picture looked like disturbed snow, and he probably wouldn't get much better quality than a small flurry no matter how hard he tried. It didn't really matter anyway, since he mainly used the television for ambient sound when he cooked.

"Hey, Bran," Dillon began, trying to keep his voice neutral. His throat was dry, making it hard to swallow.

"Hay is for horses, Dillon," Brannigan responded as usual. He tipped one of the antennas half an inch to the left with one finger as he twirled one end of his dark, handlebar mustache with the other. He'd always reminded Dillon, in looks, of an evil villain or the strong man at the circus. But despite his rough exterior, the man could make a mean Guinness cake.

"Yeah, well, we have a few new horses in the barn."

The other man glanced up. "New customers?" He straightened to his full six feet. "What are they wantin'?"

Dillon's gaze skirted away, focusing on the bandanna crumpled to smithereens in his hands. "They, uh, haven't ordered yet. And I'm not feeling too hot." His throat was dry after all. He looked up, hoping desperation wasn't written all over his face. "Maybe you could…"

Brannigan stared at him for a moment before brushing past his shoulder and taking a peek into the main room. He let out a low chuckle before slapping him on the back. "What? Are ye afraid of girls?"

"No! I just—"

The pub owner shoved him toward the door. "I'm the cook, lad. I have my job, and you have yours. Now do it."

Fine.

Ignoring his boss, Dillon smoothed out the bandanna and tied it around his head in a few hard tugs. The cloth covered most of his dark, wavy hair.

"What are you doin'?" Bran asked, amusement etched in his voice.

"My job." Grabbing a notebook and pencil from the pocket of his apron, he pushed through the door and entered the main room of the pub.

The three young people were still engrossed in lively conversation as he headed their way. Good. Maybe he'd be just another faceless server to them, and all of this would be over in half an hour.

He reached their table. "What can I be getting you today?" And guess who just spoke with an Irish accent? Disguise was more than just clothing.

The group stopped talking and zeroed in on his face. He struggled to keep a pleasant—and unrecognizable—expression.

"Hi!" One of the girls shot him a smile, her red ponytail bobbing as she practically bounced in her seat. "I'm Kaylee, and I'll just have a coffee with cream. It's too cold outside to eat."

The guy laughed. "What kind of logic is that?"

She wrinkled her nose at him. "I'm from Florida, Clark. Even in January our temps can reach the 80s. I'm shivering so much I think I'd get motion sickness if I ate right now."

"Well, I'm from Southern California, and I'll have the shepherd's pie and coffee. Black." Clark shoved his black frames up the bridge of his nose, and Dillon couldn't help but think he was pushing the Clark Kent angle a bit on the heavy side, complete with messenger bag and a Superman-blue pullover sweater.

After he jotted down the first two orders, he raised his head to find the last girl staring at him with intensity than made a muscle in his jaw twitch. He forced a smile. "And what will you have?"

"Tea." Her lips barely moved as she continued to study him

like he was an elusive answer on an exam. She was pretty. Delicate features with silky black hair framing a dark face. Eyes the color of caramel candy.

Pretty. But that didn't mean he didn't want to get the heck away from her as soon as possible. He recalled what Bran had said about him being afraid of girls.

"Tea," he repeated. "That all?"

She blinked. "And stew."

"Stew." He wrote it down. "Gotcha. Will bring 'em right out when they're done."

Dillon had almost reached the kitchen door when he heard Kaylee's loud whisper, "Arielle, you were staring him down. Do you think he's cute?"

If only that were the case.

When he returned with their drinks, they looked up from their close huddle with expectant expressions. He almost made a run for it then and there. He recognized those looks, though he hadn't encountered them in a while.

"Here you go." Setting down each of their drinks with hurried care, he turned to go when the girl, Arielle, spoke up.

"You look familiar. Did you ever live in the States?"

Dillon closed his eyes briefly before swiveling back around with fake smile. "Sorry?"

"You're right, Ari." Kaylee leaned toward him, almost coming out of her chair. Apparently personal space wasn't her thing. "I know I've seen him somewhere."

Clark rolled his eyes. "Kay, give the guy some room to breathe." He gave Dillon an apologetic glance.

"So?" Arielle persisted. "Have you been to the States before?"

"No." Straight up lie.

She sagged back in her chair as Kaylee continued to scrutinize him with sparkling eyes. "Maybe you were in a movie filmed here in Ireland? That's it, isn't it?" She engaged her companions with her active gaze. "I know I've seen someone that looks like him on TV or the internet."

Arielle's face lit up.

Oh, no.

"Yeah…" She drew out the word as pieces seemed to click together in her head.

"I've never been outside of Ireland before." What was it—lies come before a fall? No, that's pride. Maybe they were the same thing.

"You look like that Sanders guy." Surprise. Clark was the one who finally spit it out.

Dillon's heart jolted in his chest. He wanted to rip the glasses off the dude's face and expose his deepest, darkest secrets.

"Yes!" Kaylee practically shouted, shoving her pointer finger into Clark's face. "One of the Sanders boys." Relaxing back in her chair, she released a sigh as if she'd run a marathon and could now rest. "They're so hot." She snapped her gaze back to Dillon, her cheeks blooming a shade of red that rivaled her hair color. "I mean…not that you—but you are—just—"

"What Sanders guy?" Dillon blurted out. No matter how many cracks were showing in this glass charade, he just had to keep going. Why couldn't he just find some way to casually change the subject? And leave.

The three Americans gaped at him like he was an alien from Jupiter and not the Irishman he pretended to be.

"You don't know anything about the Sanders family?" Arielle asked, voice thick with skepticism. "They're famous. As in, known worldwide. They have their thumbs in every pie. Politics, healthcare, education, entertainment, and, of course, hospitality, which started it all."

Technically, the only ties his family had to politics and entertainment were his step-cousin, Ryan, who worked for the IRS, and Aunt Brenda, who was a recurring character on a daytime soap. But, hey, family is family.

"They are more well-known in America," Clark pointed out.

"Do they *have* to do with the Sanders Hotels?" Dillon realized his jaw was getting sore from grinding his teeth together and attempted to relax the muscles in his face. He really needed to get back to the kitchen.

"So you have heard of them." Arielle looked satisfied he proved himself not to be a complete moron.

Kaylee nodded, a dreamy smile crossing her face. "They're considered American royalty." Her expression dampened. "Too bad the only two Sanders boys close to my age are unavailable. I'd so marry into that family." She ticked reasons off her fingers. "Rich, good-looking, smart, super nice, and—"

"Full of tragedy," Clark interjected before taking a swig of his coffee.

Dillon's chest tightened.

"But still, the eldest found a Cinderella love story despite what his family is going through the past two years. The released footage of the wedding was gorgeous."

Wait, Parker was married? When had that happened? The tension in his body released a smidge. At least his brother had found some happiness.

"And the younger brother is the 'Prodigal Son.'" Arielle used air quotes to emphasis the words. She let out a disgusted breath. "A real prize he is, running off when his family needed him the most. Right after his mom's horrible accident, and now—"

"Dillon!" Brannigan bellowed from the kitchen. "Food's ready!"

A sheet of ice-cold sweat slid down his back. For the third time in less than fifteen minutes, the others turned in tandem to stare fiery holes through his façade.

Kaylee's brow crimped. "You're name's Dillon? Like…Dillon Sanders?"

He shrugged, surprising even himself by his casual attitude. Comfortable with playing a part. "Coincidence?" His fake accent slipped.

Dang four-syllable word.

Pivoting on his heel, he strode back into the kitchen, pushing past Brannigan who was ready to hand him the plates of food. He tore off his apron and bandanna as he headed for the back stairs leading to his rented room above the pub.

"Dillon?"

"You'll have to serve them, Bran, I quit."

By the time he reached his room, his heart raced, and his hands were vibrating from remaining clenched tight for such a long period of time. As he pulled out his backpack from beneath the bed, he didn't know if he was breathing hard from fear, anger, or simply frustration. He kicked the bedpost, almost surprised the rickety piece didn't crumble beneath the force.

Three and a half months. The longest he'd stayed in one place after over two years of traveling from place to place, looking over his shoulder, and praying he wouldn't be seen or recognized. Well, not actually praying. He and God weren't on speaking terms at the moment.

He thought he'd finally found a place to settle for a while. He was a fool for hoping.

Brannigan entered the room right when Dillon tossed his last article of clothing into the bag and zipped it shut. "What do ye think you're doin'?"

"I'm sorry, Bran, but I have to leave." He would have left right then if the pub owner's bulk hadn't filled the entire doorway. Looking the closest person he could call a friend in two years in the eye, he said, "Do you remember when I first came here, and you told me you didn't care where I've been and where I'm going, but I was welcome as long as it was today?"

After a slight hesitation, Brannigan nodded.

"Thank you, but it's tomorrow now, and I've worn out my welcome." Dillon straightened his shoulders. "I have to be on my way."

The older man touched the edge of his mustache but refrained from twirling. "Did you know the name 'Dillon' has an Irish history?"

"Yes, my…" He cast his gaze to the side, "mom told me. She has some Irish ancestors."

"Ah, well, do you know the Dillon motto then?"

A motto? He shook his head.

"*Dum Spiro, Spero*. It means 'while I breathe, I hope.'"

Dillon shifted the weight of his bag onto his other shoulder, strangely moved but shoving the feeling away. "Why are you telling me this?"

Bran placed a hand on his shoulder, forcing Dillon to look straight into his compassionate gaze. "Because, lad, sometimes I think you forget to breathe."

Releasing his grip, Bran moved to the side, allowing Dillon to pass through the doorway. And leave.

Each friend represents a world in us, a world possibly not born until they arrive, and it is only by this meeting that a new world is born.

–Anais Nin

CHAPTER TWO

Two lights.

Pinpricks in the darkness growing steadily larger with each breath he took. His heart raced, but he wasn't frightened.

The rumble of a car's engine vibrated the air, sending shivers down his spine.

Planting his feet firmly in the middle of the road, he spread his arms wide in surrender.

He wouldn't run. He deserved this.

A child's laughter cut through the air, catching him off guard. So innocent, so joyful.

His stance wavered.

The child appeared in front of him, twirling. Her long hair and flowing dress swirled around her in the lights of the approaching vehicle.

No. This was wrong. She wasn't supposed to be here.

Move. The word caught in his throat, almost strangling him.

The headlights grew closer, but the child seemed unaware, dancing in the middle of the road.

Move! Again, he couldn't push the word out, nor could he move his body.

Heart thundering in his chest, the screech of the car's skidding tires seemed far away as the girl finally faced him. He caught a glimpse of bright, hazel eyes filled with life before headlights flashed across his vision, and the world turned white.

~*~

Ring! Ring!
Dillon groaned and pulled the pillow over his head. The dank scent of old feathers only served to wake him further.
Ring! Ring!
He cracked open one eye, surveying the tiny room he had rented in a questionable bed and breakfast nestled in the heart of bustling London, England. Thankfully, it was still dark outside or he was sure the pounding in his head due to his hangover and intensely vivid dream would have turned into a full-fledged migraine.
Ring! Ring!
Mumbling about bad service and aspirin, Dillon reached for the antique phone on the bedside table. "H-hello?" he murmured, his face still half-buried in his pillow.

"Dillon Sanders?" a woman asked on the other end. "Is this Dillon?"

Still half-asleep, he answered without thinking. "Yes, this is Dillon." He yawned.

"Oh, thank goodness, I finally reached you!" the woman exclaimed. "I don't know if you remember me, but this is Fiona Miller. I used to be your babysitter."

It took a few seconds for Fiona's words to sink in, but when they did Dillon sat up with a start, causing a streak of pain to rocket through his head. He let out a low groan.

"Are-are you alright?" she asked uncertainly.

"No, I'm not," he snapped. He drew in a ragged breath and ran his fingers through bedraggled hair. "How did you get this number, Ms. Fi?"

"You do remember me!" She sounded way too delighted for Dillon's taste, but then again, she always was excited easily. "I've tried a few numbers now, but thank the Lord, we finally found you."

Dillon pressed the heel of his hand against his pounding head. He should hang up. But who had given her a 'few numbers' to call? Brannigan? No, Bran didn't even know who he really was. The faces of the college kids from the week before flitted through his mind. Was he being tailed?

Fiona's words suddenly registered in his fogged brain.

"We?" Dread wormed its way into his stomach. "Who's 'we'?"

"Just your Grandad and me." Fiona's words and more subdued tone was a blessing, to say the least. Her voice lowered further. "Your grandfather is the reason I called you, Dillon."

His grip tightened. He should really hang up.

"A little less than a year ago, he was diagnosed with cancer. He went through radiation and chemo, but…" Fiona paused to sigh, and when she continued, she sounded older. "He moved back to Mobile from Atlanta in November and decided to stay in Sanders

24

Nursing Home. I think it makes him feel closer to your grand-mother. I'm your Grandad's private nurse, and the past month, he's grown progressively worse, until he's at the point where…" She drifted off again.

"He's dying," Dillon finished, his voice hollow. He'd known since the moment she started speaking. Her next comments faded to a blur though he caught that the doctors only expected Grandad to survive just a few more weeks.

He fervently wished the sun was out, because the dark of the night seemed to seep into his pores and grip his soul.

Fiona's next words were expected, but they caused him to flinch nonetheless. "Your Grandad's last wish is to see you again. To speak with you. Will you come?"

"Um—" He yanked a hard hand through his tousled hair as he stalled. "Are-are my dad and Parker there?"

"No, but I believe they're planning to come as soon as their schedules allow."

Dillon's head pounded, and his stomach churned. Decisions. It was time to make one.

"Yes." The answer tumbled out, causing his heart to race. He quickly added, "On one condition. Don't let anyone else in my family know I'm coming."

"Okay," Fiona promised. "I understand. And thank you. You have no idea how much this will—"

Dillon dropped the receiver and rushed to the bathroom. He barely made it before he lost all the contents of his stomach. He heaved twice before he was able to stop.

Slumping on the cold tiles, he mentally added up how much it would cost to buy a ticket to Mobile, Alabama. At least he didn't run the chance of running into his dad and brother.

He still couldn't believe he'd be spending the last of his money on family when he swore he'd never have anything to do with them again. But then again, this was Grandad. He was dying.

Those college kids were right. His family was full of tragedy. How much more could they take before collapsing completely?

He was sure his secret would be the straw that broke the camel's back.

Dillon gripped the edge of the toilet and squeezed his eyes shut as he fought another wave of nausea and grief welling up in his chest.

He would just have to stay invisible. And keep his silence.

When his flight landed at 10:05 at night, Fiona was waiting to pick him up in the Mobile Regional Airport parking lot like they planned. He winced when he saw her dressed very non-incognito with spiky red-dyed hair and smiley-face covered scrubs. She looked like a neon sign. At least maybe she drew attention from him in his jeans and plain gray, hooded jacket.

The moment she laid eyes on him, his old babysitter walked toward him with open arms and damp eyes.

Dillon stiffened as Fiona embraced him, squeezing so tight he was sure he'd have dents in his upper arms.

"It's so wonderful to see you again," she whispered tearfully.

He gave her an awkward pat on the shoulder. It'd been a while since someone had hugged him. "You too, Ms. Fi." Darting furtive looks over her head, he made sure no one was watching. "Can we get in the car now?"

Fiona immediately released him, laughing as she pulled out an embroidered handkerchief to pat the corners of her eyes. "So sorry! Just get emotional, you know." She shot him a bright smile, motioning for him to toss his bag in the back seat. "Hop in."

During the twenty-minute drive from the airport to downtown Mobile, Fiona only attempted to make conversation twice before realizing her passenger didn't have anything to say. She turned on the radio to a Christian station and softly sang along.

Dillon distracted himself from his whirling thoughts by focusing on the passing scenery. The openness of West Mobile eventually melted into the bustle of the ever-growing city. Since it was later at night, they didn't have as much traffic holding them up. Eventually, they reached Government Street which led them toward the heart of Mobile, a true mix of old and new.

He and his dad, mom, and brother used to come to Mobile to visit his dad's parents every Christmas, and during the summer, they'd pass through the city on the way to their condo in Gulf Shores. A lot of his childhood memories were in this city.

Then Grandma passed away six years ago, and Dillon's dad, Jacob, convinced Grandad to move to Atlanta so he could be closer to them. Dillon hadn't been back since.

As they entered downtown and passed a tall building constructed of dark red brick with black wrought iron embellishments, he sank back into his seat and tugged the hood of his jacket further over his forehead. His heart pounded as he caught the words printed in bold script on the awning.

Sanders Hotel. Established 1943.

It was the flagship hotel that began an empire. During World War II, his great-grandfather, Thomas, couldn't fight because of his crippled legs due to having polio as a child. But his desire to help somehow was great and despite coming out of the Great Depression and being knee-deep in war, his parents still had a good amount of money they left him when they passed.

Thomas used his inheritance to build an affordable yet luxury-filled hotel for the influx of people who'd moved to Mobile to work in the shipyards and air field. After the war, the hotel continued to thrive under Thomas' hand and became well-known for their hospitality, comfort, and service. Eventually, as his children grew up and helped with the business, other Sanders Hotels were built across the nation and then the world. Their family dynasty was sealed.

Dillon breathed a little easier as they passed the hotel even as his stomach tightened. His great-grandfather had multiplied his inheritance, blessing his family. He simply sucked the life out of his.

"Here we are!" Fiona's bright voice seemed even louder than usual after their conversation-less car ride.

Climbing out of the car, he stared up at the four-story, white and tan nursing home with palm trees lining the walkway leading up to the front entrance. His gaze veered toward a window on the third floor where a soft light glowed. Grandma's old room. "You think Grandad moved here to feel closer to her?"

Fiona motioned for him to follow her. Light from the half-moon overhead lit her soft expression. "I know he did. Knit at the soul those two were."

They entered through the automatic glass doors into the spacious lobby, and Dillon struggled not to hold his breath.

He'd always hated the smell of hospitals and nursing homes. That mix of disinfectant and illness. It never failed to make him shudder and want to shun all healthcare facilities, which he supposed was ironic, considering his great-grandfather also founded Sanders Memorial Hospital which Sanders Nursing Home was affiliated, and his mother had been a philanthropist whose concentration was to better healthcare.

"Fiona!" A middle-aged woman in flowered scrubs hurried toward them from one of the adjacent halls. "Thank goodness you're here!"

Dillon turned so he wasn't facing her, pretending to peruse a mural of a park scene painted on the wall. She didn't even seem to notice him.

"Penny," Fiona said, "what's wrong?"

The woman, Penny, rambled on about one of the other nurses

having to leave because her child was sick and how one of the patients, Mrs. Johansson, was being a handful again and they needed someone to watch after her right away until the new shift started.

Dillon could practically feel Fiona's eyes boring into the back of his head as she wavered in her decision.

"Of course, I'll be there right away." After Penny thanked her profusely and ran off, Fiona placed a warm hand on Dillon's back. "Why don't you head on up and visit your Grandad? You don't need me there anyway. I'll come check up on you two as soon as I can." She gestured toward the elevator. "Third floor and to your left. You'll know where."

"Okay." Dillon watched his old babysitter disappear down one of the hallways, feeling strangely bereft.

Muscles in his back and neck coiled with tension as he stepped into the elevator and pressed the button for the third floor.

It was quiet. Not even the annoying elevator music was playing. You'd think he would be used to silence after living alone for so long, but right now, he'd have done anything to be sitting in a rowdy pub in Ireland, invisible in the noise.

The elevator doors slid open with a quiet ding and he stepped into the hallway.

The sound of trickling water from a fountain mounted on the wall directly across from Dillon soothed his nerves a bit. He'd almost forgotten about the fountains on each floor that greeted anyone who stepped off the elevators.

Water symbolized healing, replenishing, and peace. At least, according to Dillon's mom, Carol. After Grandma died, she had kept a special eye on the nursing home. The fountains were her idea.

Dillon walked over to the fountain and watched trickles of water run over the indentions of a ceramic clam shell and waterfall into a small pool beneath. He slid his hand beneath the shell and felt the cool streams wash over his fingers before continuing their journey to the pool of clear water below. At least twenty or more coins could be seen lying at the bottom of the fountain.

Wishes, he thought.

Prayers, Mom would say.

The metallic clunk of a can dropping in a soda machine startled him away from the water's mesmerizing calm. He glanced to his right toward the waiting room at the far end of the hall as he dried his hand on his shirt. The soda and snack machines usually were around the corner. His stomach churned at the thought of eating anything at the moment.

Squaring his shoulders, he strode down the hall in the opposite direction of the waiting room until he reached the first closed door on his left. Grandma's old room.

Raising a hand to knock, he noticed it trembling slightly. He rolled his fingers into a fist and rapped on the door.

When no one responded, he turned the doorknob and poked his head inside. A frown grew on his face as he pushed the door open further and stepped into the room.

The familiar steady beep of a heart monitor filled the air, and light from a corner lamp illuminated a person lying in a hospital bed. A person who was definitely not Grandad.

It was a girl.

They say a person needs just three things to be truly happy in this world.
Someone to love, something to do, and something to hope for.
—Tom Bodett

CHAPTER THREE

Natalie

"Sorry I've been gone so long, Beth." Natalie plugged a few coins into the nursing home's snack machine and punched in an order of Peanut M&M's. Her reflection stared back at her from the snack machine's window as she waited for the spiral to release the yellow package.

Dark smudges were under her eyes, making her cheeks look even more pale than usual. Bedraggled, shoulder-length brown strands of hair escaped from a loose ponytail. Definitely not the look of the successful, stylish journalist she aspired to become.

Natalie's business partner, mentor, and friend, Bethany Lane, huffed into the other end of the phone. "Really, Nat, the accident just happened, what? Almost three weeks ago?"

"Two weeks and three days."

"Yeah, well—" Natalie could almost hear Beth's sarcastic eye roll, "—I can understand why you need some time off. You can finish some of your articles from Mobile, you know."

"I know, but, I mean, we just started the magazine together, and I just want to come, because…" Her words jumbled together as she grabbed the M&M's and bought a Diet Coke from the soda machine.

"You need a break?" That was Beth, always cutting right to the heart of a matter.

Natalie winced, gripping the cold soda can while the package of M&M's dangled from her fingers. She opened her mouth to object, but a rejected sigh escaped instead. "Maybe."

"Then come on up. I don't mean to sound harsh, but there's not much you can do right now."

"I know…" She kicked the base of the soda machine lightly with the toe of her suede, ankle boot.

"Fiona can call you if there's any change." Beth paused. "From what you tell me about your sister, she'd understand."

Would she? Natalie tilted her head upwards, staring blindly at the ceiling. She didn't know anymore. She didn't know anything anymore.

"I'll think about it. Probably. Maybe."

Beth laughed. "Well, as long as you're sure. Hey, it's getting late here, and I have an interview to conduct early tomorrow, so I've gotta go."

"I'll text you when I decide. I think I'll talk to Parker first."

"Sounds good. Night."

"Good night." Natalie tapped the End button and scrolled through her contacts until she found her husband's name.

Parker Sanders. The Golden Boy of America.

Her Golden Boy.

Natalie's throat tightened. She missed him. Married for a little over two weeks and they'd barely spent three days together as husband and wife.

True, he was pretty much running a multi-million dollar enterprise. His fierce dedication to his family legacy was one of the things that drew Natalie to him in the first place. They both were workaholics to some degree, passionate about their careers, so they understood each other in that respect.

They called, texted, and Skyped every day, and he'd flown down every chance he got.

Still, she missed him.

She even wore one of Parker's jackets. It helped her feel less homesick for him. Bringing the edge of the jacket up to her nose, she breathed in deeply. Though faint, Parker's scent—sweet and earthy—filled her senses.

Realizing what she was doing, Natalie straightened, glancing around. But thankfully no one was around to watch her moon over her husband's jacket.

She glanced at Parker's name again on the phone's screen before stuffing it back into her pocket. He always went to bed early. She'd call him in the morning.

The nursing home's halls had grown familiar over the past couple weeks. She was up there every day, and spent most of her nights there too.

After stuffing the M&M's in the jacket pocket, Natalie headed back up the hall. She popped open the Diet Coke and took a long swig, almost choking on the carbonation. She swallowed hard. Her eyes burned.

Stopping in the empty hallway, she forced herself to take deep, even breaths. She really wished she could go on a run. Anything to get away from the stress and guilt weighing her down.

But she couldn't run right now. She had done enough running in the past and promised herself she was done.

She was done. That was it. She'd stay. She had to. Didn't she?

Natalie took another sip of her Coke, this time a tiny sip, and as she continued walking she shot up a quick prayer. *Lord, I'm so overwhelmed. What should I do now?* It's a prayer she'd recited so often she wondered if God ever tired of her asking.

When her sister's room came into view, she froze. The door was open, but she was positive she'd closed it. Heart racing, she jogged to the doorway then stopped short when she saw a young man standing inside the room.

"What are you doing?" Her voice came out like a hiss.

The young man jumped and turned around. He looked awful. His blue eyes were bloodshot, and his dark brown hair looked like he had run his fingers through it a bit too many times.

"How did you get in here?" Natalie demanded as she strode toward him. She clenched her soda can and heard it crinkle. "Do you have family here? Because, if you do, then you have the wrong room."

The guy took a step back as she barricaded herself between him and the hospital bed. He ran a hand through his hair. "S-sorry," he stuttered. "I didn't—I mean—" His eyes fluttered closed for a brief second as he sighed. "This was a mistake," he whispered. He cast a glance over her shoulder at the hospital bed, eyes shadowed, before backing away.

As he turned, a muscle ticked in his jaw, and Natalie caught a glimpse of his profile. She caught her breath.

"Wait."

He froze but didn't look at her.

Natalie eased toward him. "Are you looking for Parker?"

The guy shot her a startled look. "Parker?"

"Yeah," she said slowly. When he just stared at her, Natalie was able to look more closely at his features, noting his strong chin and sensitive eyes, and she was sure of it. "Dillon, right?"

He furrowed his brow. "How did—"

"You look so much like your brother," she replied. "I'm Natalie Griggs, well, Sanders now. Parker's wife." She let out a short, humorless laugh. "I understand if you don't recognize me, since, well, we never met and you didn't come to the wedding and all…"

Understanding dawned in Dillon's eyes followed immediately by embarrassment then puzzlement. "Wait…Natalie—what are you doing here?" He shot an anxious look toward the door. "Is anyone else with you?"

She frowned. "You don't know…" Her voice trailed off as she realized that of course he wouldn't know. She had begged Parker and his father to keep quiet about the details, but she had forgotten just how big the estrangement between Dillon and his family had been.

Leveling her gaze on her newly discovered brother-in-law, Natalie tried to remember all Parker had said about him. Dillon was smart. Parker had mentioned how his younger brother had been in all honors classes in high school and would have been valedictorian is he hadn't left home his senior year when he was around seventeen.

But that was the only nice thing Parker had ever said about his brother. That was only thing. Period. Besides explaining how Dillon had disappeared one day with only a note saying not to follow him. He'd left his dad and brother to deal with the aftereffects of his mother's awful accident.

Natalie pursed her lips. She couldn't feel the same bitterness toward him she suspected Parker felt. She knew what it was like choosing to separate oneself from their family. She had done it. Her own mother had done it. Though she was a bit late to change some things, Natalie had returned home. Maybe Dillon was too.

Wait. If he didn't know…

"Why are you here?" she asked. "After all this time?"

Dillon looked at his feet, seeming reluctant to answer. He finally peeked up at her through his mess of hair. "You know Grandad, right?"

A smile slid onto her face, and it was a relief. She hadn't cracked a true smile in a couple days. "Yes, of course, I know Grandad."

"Well, I got a call a little while ago from Ms. Fi—Fiona—who told me that Grandad was—that he's—" Dillon straightened and blew out his breath. "I didn't—" His voice was tight.

Against her better judgment, her heart went out to him. "He's down the hall. Third door on your left."

Dillon gave her a searching look. "Thanks," he finally said but didn't move. His gaze went over her shoulder again and lingered. "Who is she?"

Natalie turned and followed his gaze. Light from the hallway and the lamp in the corner bathed the sixteen-year-old girl in a soft glow. Wavy, blondish-brown hair spread nice and neat across her pillow. Her chest rose and fell in a beautiful, steady rhythm with help from a breathing machine.

"She's my sister."

"Your sister?" Dillon asked incredulously as Natalie moved to take a seat beside the bed.

"How—why—" He cleared his throat. "I'm sorry."

She nodded. "Yeah."

"So," he lowered himself into a chair on the other side of the bed, "what happened?"

Natalie's stomach clenched, but she calmly threaded her fingers through her sister's and stroked the back of her hand. "She's been in a coma ever since my wedding over two weeks ago."

"Overdo it on the Cha Cha slide?"

She shot him a startled look.

He winced. "Sorry, I didn't mean—"

"No," she interrupted. To her surprise, she started to laugh. "No." She gasped, trying to control herself. Taking a deep breath, she focused on her sister's face.

Get it together, Nat.

"No," she said again. "Not the Cha Cha Slide." Though her baby sister did love to dance.

Except for the hospital machines, silence filled the room. It wasn't uncomfortable though. In fact, it was kind of nice.

Natalie let her mind go blank, void of any particular thought, until Dillon spoke up again.

"I guess I should go see Grandad." Reluctance and longing were evident in his raw voice. "And, Natalie, if you could not—"

Fiona barreled into the room, looking out of breath. Her rapid gaze flicked between them. "Oh. Oh, dear."

Natalie quickly surmised the situation. "Fiona…did you know about Dillon coming?"

Dillon answered for her. "She did." He attempted to give the woman a hard look but failed. Obviously, there was affection between them. "You told me none of my family would be here, Ms. Fi."

She shook her head, a suspicious twinkle in her eye. "No, you asked if Parker or your father were here, and I said no. You said nothing of a sister-in-law."

Natalie bit her lip to keep from smiling as Dillon rolled his eyes and pushed to his feet.

"So can I see Grandad now?"

Wringing her hands, Fiona gave him an imploring look. "I just checked in on him, and he's asleep. It's been days since he's truly gotten a good night's rest."

"Of course he chooses tonight," Dillon muttered.

Fiona gave him a firm stare that caused him to duck his head in repentance.

Natalie wondered what the history was between the two when she remembered Parker once mentioning that Fiona used to be their babysitter.

"Could you wait until morning?" Fiona asked.

"Here?"

"You could stay at the Sanders Hotel," Natalie suggested then immediately regretted it when she saw his face blanch. His obvious refusal to associate with anyone connected to his family besides Grandad should have tipped her off the hotel was off-limits too. "Or you could stay here, in this room. I was going to sleep on the cot over there, but you can. I've slept sitting up a lot recently."

Dillon shifted his feet, looking for all the world like he wanted to bolt out the door like a cat with its tail on fire. Glancing from Natalie to her sister to Fiona and the door, he sagged like the fire inside him was extinguished, fatigue etched in his face. "Fine. I'll stay the night."

Fiona clapped her hands together once. "Wonderful! Oh, Dillon—"

"But—" he interrupted, pinning each of them with a hard glare edged with desperation. "You two have to promise not to contact anyone about my being here."

A bubble of irritation rose in Natalie's chest. "I can't lie to my husband."

"At least don't tell him anything until after I leave town." He ran his hand through his hair just like Parker did when he was stressed or upset. "Please?"

Her heart softened. She sank back into her seat and took a sip of Coke before responding. "Okay."

Fiona agreed.

Dillon gave a stiff nod. "Okay."

Promising to return in the morning, Fiona left, leaving Natalie and Dillon in a tense silence.

"Um, I can sleep in the chair," he offered.

"I'm guessing you just flew a number of hours on an airplane sitting up. It's fine. You can take the cot."

Dillon didn't argue. He settled on the cot sitting a couple feet away from the foot of the hospital bed. A deep sigh escaped him as he sank back onto the pillow without pulling the covers over him. He looked like a little boy who'd just spent the day running a marathon.

Natalie's journalist instincts begged her to ask him a dozen questions, but her sisterly instincts told her to wait.

Two young people lay before her. One sister and now a new brother. Both broken. And she had no idea how she could help mend them. But she had to try.

"What's her name?"

Shaking away her thoughts, she looked up to see Dillon staring at the girl in the hospital bed, an unreadable expression on his face.

"Hope," Natalie replied. She dug in Parker's jacket pocket, pulled out the packet of Peanut M&M's, and ripped open the top. "Her name is Hope."

The soul is a garden enclosed, our own perpetual paradise where we can be refreshed and restored.
—Thomas Moore

CHAPTER FOUR

Hope

The first thing I noticed was the fragrance.

Rich, though not overpowering. Light and fresh. Sweet.

A gentle breeze brushed my cheeks, prompting me to open my eyes and blink several times.

I lay inside a gazebo. The ceiling spiraled above me like a tepee or a castle turret.

Random diamonds of light poked through white lattice work covered in honeysuckle vines.

Drawing in a long breath, I again noticed the intoxicating fragrance. It couldn't just be the honeysuckles that produced that kind of scent. I could practically taste the sweetness on my tongue.

Curiosity piqued, I sat up to get a better look at my surroundings.

The gazebo had four open doorways, each one revealing a view of a garden. But not just any garden. *The* garden.

My peach-colored skirt flowed in silken waves over my legs as I stood and slowly walked to the closest entrance. Bracing my hand against the doorframe, I stared, mesmerized.

In the distance, a line of dark green trees ringed the edge of the garden, but in between me and the trees spread a landscape so lush and colorful, my eyes couldn't take it all in at once. Flowers of all shapes, sizes, and textures grew in abundance. Rich dirt pathways tangled through the flowering plants like strings of various necklaces dripping with priceless jewels. A single, crystal thread of a stream wound its way through all the colors.

Butterflies with wings like stained glass fluttered to and fro. Dragonflies zipped by like liquid silver. The cheerful lilt of birds singing could be heard nearby.

My eyes fluttered closed as I stood as still as a statue. Another breeze blew through the doorway behind me, twirling strands of hair around my face. Still, I didn't move. I just breathed.

In and out. In. Out.

That's when I heard it.

Someone singing. And coming closer.

I gasped, my eyelids flying open. The realization that I was probably trespassing on someone's private property speared through me. They would be so mad if they found me here. I hated making people angry.

Frantically swiveling my head, I searched for a place to hide.

The singing was louder now, and I knew I couldn't leave the gazebo without someone noticing me, so I pressed myself into a curve of one of the gazebo's walls and sank to the floor. Drawing my knees to my chest, I tried to become as small as possible. My eyes squeezed shut as I held my breath.

The singer was a man. I could tell that now though I couldn't see him. His voice was deep and pure and…happy.

Slowly, my eyes opened as I listened.

He was really close now. Probably on the other side of the wall I was leaning against.

His words floated clearly through the gazebo's lattice work:

Come away, come away,
Come away with me!
I went away, went away,
Went away to the garden.

Here you are found,
Are found, are found.
Where flowers bloom
And awaken, awaken!

It sounded like he was about to break into laughter as he sang. I had never heard anyone that happy before.

I pulled myself to my feet, trying to be careful not to make a noise. Holding my breath, I rose until I could peek between the lattice work and honeysuckle vines. I was looking down on the man's back.

He was bent over inspecting the closed buds of various flowers surrounding him. The sleeves of his loose, white shirt were rolled up, revealing strong, tanned arms. His longish, dark hair was pulled back with a strip of leather. He must have been the gardener.

Suddenly, he stood up. I almost gasped, but he didn't seem to notice me.

Flinging his arms open, he looked ready to embrace the sky as he spun around with inherent grace and pounded his feet against the earth in a rhythmic heartbeat of a dance. His voice rolled out like powerful ocean waves, drawing me in.

A time, a season,
A feeling, a face.
A weakness, a strength,
A healing place.

I clamped my hands over my mouth, my eyes growing wide when the closed flower buds around him began unfurling and bursting open in a kaleidoscope display. Who was this man who could awaken flowers with his voice?

It was breath-taking. It was a bit terrifying.

Come away, come away,
Come away with me!
In the garden, the garden,
Alive I'll be!

Pressing my lips tightly together, I took a step backwards and darted my gaze toward the entrance farthest away from the gardener. The line of trees stood in the distance. Refuge?

I cast one more glance through the lattice to make sure he was still distracted before silently backing up toward my escape route.

A large splinter pierced my foot. Wincing silently, I reached down to tug it out when I saw them. Ugly scratches and cuts, some faint, some fairly deep, but all dark red with dried blood covered the soles of my feet and the palms of my hands. A faint memory of falling and icy glass piercing my skin flittered through my mind.

Unbidden tears clouded my vision as a shaky gasp escaped my lips.

The gardener stopped singing.

For a moment there was complete silence. Then I panicked.

Jerking around, I sprinted out of the gazebo. My feet kicked up dirt as I ran down one of the winding paths I too late realized curved away toward my left—away from the trees. I groaned, a sudden hitch forming in my side.

I spotted a group of azalea bushes nearby. Making a snap decision, I dove behind them, trying to still my ragged breaths and listening to hear if he had followed me.

As my breathing quieted, I peered between the wide leaves of the bushes. I could see the gardener in the gazebo doorway I had just fled through. He stood with his hands relaxed on his hips and looking in my direction, his gaze passing over the bushes but not lingering.

He stayed there for what felt like an eternity before turning around. And leaving. He was leaving.

I just lay in the dirt, surprised I didn't feel relieved.

But then he called over his shoulder, "If you want to come out of hiding, I'd enjoy your company." He walked away.

After a few moments, he began to sing.

Philosophy is really nostalgia, the desire to be at home.
Novalis

CHAPTER FIVE

Parker

Parker knew it was time to stop working when the words on the computer screen blurred into an unreadable mass.

Stretching back in his office chair, he blinked hard to restore some moisture to his eyes. A glance at the time told him he'd stayed way past overtime. Usually, he went to bed early, but the past couple nights his routine had changed. Of course, a Vice CEO's work is never done.

At least, that's what he told himself.

The truth was, he didn't want to head back to his apartment. He may be called a sap, but he hated being alone. Being around people, especially those he cared about, gave him energy. With Nat, the one person he cared about most, still in Mobile, their new place practically echoed with emptiness and left him feeling restless.

After saving the document he'd been typing, Parker shut off the computer and headed out, deciding some Chinese sounded good.

Like his father, Parker had an office on the second floor of Sanders Hotel Atlanta and often floated between the hotel and their main offices downtown, but he preferred actually working out of the hotel, the beating heart of their hospitality business.

Tonight, instead of heading out the back elevator, he decided to go down the front stairs and through the lobby.

Pausing at the top of the staircase, a sick feeling curled in Parker's stomach. Wrapping his fingers around the wrought iron railing, he silently counted the twenty steps that gradually widened until they reached the marble floor of the hotel foyer.

The staircase was beautiful. White marble with a carpet in a black and gold oriental pattern running down the center. It was an exact replica of the staircase in the Sanders Hotel Mobile.

The same staircase Hope fell down over two weeks ago.

Gripping the railing tighter than usual, he headed down the twenty steps, smiling and nodding to the guests and staff that greeted him. He didn't miss the curiosity that lurked in some of their eyes.

Through some pretty powerful connections, Parker and his dad were able to keep Hope's accident from becoming a media frenzy like after his mother's accident. Except for the first few days, it hadn't, and Natalie was able to tend to her sister in peace. All people knew was that she had tripped and fallen down the staircase during their wedding reception. That was all people needed to know.

Heck, that was pretty much all *he* knew.

But he also knew Natalie suspected more.

And it didn't keep people from being curious.

The buzz of his phone interrupted his thoughts. "Hello?"

"Parker," Jacob's voice filled the line, "are you still at the hotel?"

He stepped out into the Atlanta night air and pulled his coat in tighter. It was still a little brisk. "Just leaving."

"Perfect. Do you think you can stop by? I have some papers I need to go over with you."

"Sure. I'm getting some Chinese. Want anything?"

"No, I'm good. Your mother and I just had a late supper."

"Okay, see you soon."

Thirty-five minutes later and laden down with fried rice and coconut shrimp, Parker pulled through his parents' security gate and parked in the circular drive in front of the red brick colonial mansion he grew up in. He let himself in. "Hello?"

"Back here."

Parker followed the shotgun hallway and the sounds of the television until he reached the back den.

"Oh, that smells good," Jacob said as way of greeting, looking away from where Humphrey Bogart was being his suave, bitter self in Casablanca.

Rounding the brown leather couch, Parker set his bags of food on the antique trunk that served as a coffee table. "Brought plenty. You can have a midnight snack."

Leaving his dad to scavenge, Parker walked a few feet away to kiss his mother on the cheek. "Hey, Mom. How're you doing?"

Carol Sanders stared straight ahead at the TV from her position in her wheelchair but blinked her gray eyes three times, which was her answer for "Good."

"Wonderful. So is Bogart behaving himself?"

One blink. Yes.

"How about Dad?"

Two blinks. No.

Parker laughed as Jacob fake scowled around a bite of shrimp.

"Don't you listen to her. The only reason we're watching Casablanca for the thousandth time is because I'm such a nice husband."

Sitting down beside his dad, he opened another food carton. "It's a peace-offering, isn't it?"

Jacob gave his wife an affectionate smile, eyes crinkling at the corners. "Yes," he said grudgingly. "I had to cancel a visit from one of her former students today because the physical therapist could only come at the same time." He lifted his voice over the sudden swell of movie music. "I told you, Carol, I rescheduled for them to come next week."

She didn't blink.

Jacob sighed. "You know how fond she is of her students."

Parker nodded, his mouth full of fried rice.

In addition to her philanthropy projects, Carol had also worked at local high schools as a tutor and even did some summer teaching in Mobile before her accident. The pictures and letters from her students lined the walls of her study upstairs, attesting to the love she had for her students and vice versa.

While he and his father quietly discussed their paperwork, Parker brought up Mobile. "I was thinking of heading to visit Grandad and Nat this weekend."

"That sounds like a good idea." Jacob slid a glance toward Carol and lowered his voice further. "Though it's difficult for us to travel right now, I know we're probably going to head down there soon." His eyes glazed over. "With Dad being how he is…" Letting out a breath, he rubbed his hands over his face and through his brown, silver-streaked hair. "We just need to all be together as a family."

Parker tapped the end of his pen against the paper lying on his lap and wanted to mention that all of them wouldn't be there since one of them seemed to only care about himself. But the heaviness in his father's voice made it clear that he was already well-aware who was missing.

So he refrained from commenting and dove back into his family's business.

Dillon

It was the same dream again.

The car headlights drawing closer.

His resolute stance, absolute surrender to what was coming.

The joy-filled laughter came, followed by the little girl.

"You have to move!" Dillon shouted. "You aren't supposed to be here!"

She twirled like a ballerina, oblivious to him.

"No." His chest heaved. No one else was supposed to get hurt. Just him. Just him.

Only the little girl stood between him and the approaching vehicle.

"No!"

Tires screeched.

Bright, hazel eyes.

"No!" Dillon sat up with a gasp, his hand stretched outwards toward the little girl before realizing he was in the nursing home, and his hand was reaching toward the bed where Hope was laying instead.

Slowly lowering his arm, he clutched the front of his shirt and drew in a shaky breath.

It was just a dream. Just a dream.

Beams of Alabama sunlight slanted through the window to his left, lighting up the sterile room and further grounding him in reality.

Checking his watch—8:32—a large yawn stretched his mouth, causing his jaw to pop. A glance around the room told him Natalie wasn't there, which made him uneasy.

Flipping up the hood of his jacket, he scooted back and leaned against the wall. Sleep still tugged at him, jet lag to be sure, but he never could go back to sleep once the sun was up. Something he inherited from both his father and grandfather. Which meant Grandad was probably awake.

Dillon turned his face toward the window and closed his eyes, allowing the beams of sunlight soak into his skin like it was golden courage.

He reached down deep and grabbed on to his constant companion—guilt. A sigh of relief almost escaped him when his chest hollowed out, empty with pain and self-loathing. It was a familiar feeling. A safe one. It would keep him from spilling the answer to the question he knew Grandad would ask.

Natalie entered the room, typing something on her phone, and did a double-take of him sitting up. "Oh, good. You're awake."

"Where have you been?" That came out a bit more accusatory than he meant it to.

Except for raising one eyebrow, she didn't seem fazed as she returned her attention to her phone. "Not ratting you out, if that's what you're implying." She finished whatever she was doing and looked up. "Work stuff." She jerked her head toward the door. "Fiona said Grandad is awake. You ready?"

"No." Dillon stood up. "But point me where to go." Natalie told him the room number but stopped him before he could leave the room.

"Hey, when you're done, would you mind meeting me back here?" Obviously catching the wariness on his face, she rolled her eyes. "I'm not going to spring your dad or Parker on you or anything like that. I just need to ask you something."

Dillon shrugged. "Okay, fine, but I might not have an answer."

She gave his shoulder a light shove. "Just come when you're done." She returned to her business on her phone.

Once in the hallway, he noticed a couple workers and patients milling about, but they didn't pay him any attention. He'd always been able to blend into his surroundings well.

Unnoticeable. He'd never been more grateful.

Without giving himself a chance to hesitate, he walked straight into Grandad's room.

"I suppose you went to Hope's room first, huh?" That was the first thing out of Grandad's mouth when Dillon appeared in the doorway. "Don't blame you. I'd rather sleep in the same room as a pretty girl too."

Dillon stared at him a second before looking at Fiona who was standing next to Grandad's bed. "I thought you said he was at Death's door."

"You know your grandfather. Still has to speak whatever's on his mind even to his last breath." She walked over and gave him her signature strait-jacket squeeze.

With what little movement he had left, he gingerly patted her back.

Grandad wheezed as though he were the one being deprived of breath. "Let the boy go, Fi. I have something to say."

Fiona released him and wagged her pointer finger at Grandad. "You let me have my fun, Hank. I haven't seen this boy since—" She hesitated, her gaze darting back and forth between them.

Dillon felt the awkward silence in his bones.

"I suppose I should let you two talk then," Fiona finally said. "I'm going to get a drink. Would you like anything?"

He shook his head. "No, thanks, I'm good."

"I would love a root beer," Grandad piped up.

"Now, Hank, you know you aren't supposed to be drinking those." She blew each of them a kiss before she left the room.

Dillon forced a smile, shoving his hands into his pockets. "Still flirting with pretty girls, huh, Grandad?"

"So you *did* see Hope."

His smile faded. Though his grandfather put up a good face, nothing could hide the changes in his appearance.

Grandad had always been fit and lean, but the sickness seemed to have thinned him even more, making him seem almost frail. His jaw was still the same square jaw that Dillon and his brother, Parker, had inherited, but the sides of his mouth drooped slightly, causing the normally strong jaw to look weaker somehow.

His hair had changed from light gray to almost snow white since Dillon had seen him last, and it caused his blue eyes to seem brighter. Those bright blues seemed to sear through him now.

He still wore his standard plaid shirt though, and his fifty-year-old fedora he'd worn on his wedding day and to every single big occasion since sat on the bedside table on top of a Bible and a book of Shakespearean sonnets.

"How are you feeling?"

The old man raised an eyebrow, and Dillon was thrust back to a time when he could read every single one of his grandfather's facial expressions in just one glance and know what he was thinking. This look usually meant, "Are you seriously asking that question?"

A flush pricked the back of Dillon's neck. He pulled up a chair next to the bed and straddled it backwards, folding his arms across the back. Resting his chin on top of his hands, he narrowed his eyes and twisted his mouth to the side.

"Oh, I know that look." Grandad let out a raspy chuckle which transformed into a hacking cough that shook his body.

Dillon gripped the back of the chair, his knuckles turning white, until his grandfather drew in a clean breath.

"You're—" he leaned back heavily against his pillows, "—wondering what you're doing here."

"To see you. You're sick."

"Nah." He reached out and rested a cool hand on top of his grandson's head.

Dillon was surprised he didn't feel the need to flinch. In fact, he fought the urge to lean into the touch.

"Nah," Grandad said again, his voice quiet. "At least that's not the entire reason why you're here."

Dillon's eyelids weighted shut, the lump in his throat preventing him to speak. But there really wasn't a need. For several long moments, the two sat there in silence with Grandad's hand heavy on his head.

Then the unfairness of the situation almost caught him in a stranglehold and he pulled away. "You called me all the way here—"

"It was your choice."

"—when you know me well enough—"

"It was your choice."

"No!" The word shot out of his mouth like a bullet. "It was not my choice! Because no matter how far I run or how hard I hide, whether it was two years ago or now, my family keeps dragging me back. I just—just can't break free, no matter how hard I try."

Grandad's expression remained placid if not extremely pale. "Is that a bad thing?"

Dillon scrubbed his hands over his face with a groan. "Yes, Grandad, it is." Dropping his hands, he felt the familiar numbness spread through his chest. "I didn't run away just for my sake, you know."

"No, Dillon, I don't know." A sad half-grin tugged on his grandfather's lips, and he looked every bit his age plus another decade. "You don't talk to us anymore."

His throat clogged up. "No," he whispered. Rubbing his eyes with his thumb and forefinger, he let out a sigh and stood up. "And I'm sorry about that." He crossed the room and stared blindly out the window.

"Dillon," Grandad's voice was paper-thin. "I know you don't want to talk about the past, and someone would have to be blind to not see that running away has torn you up inside."

Dillon's spine straightened, but he didn't turn around.

"But I still have a favor to ask." A pause. "Turn around, son, and look at me when I'm speaking to you. Who taught you manners, anyhow?"

He faced his grandfather, caught between laughing, choking up, or punching the wall. "Mom did."

"Well, you obviously weren't a very good student."

"My teachers would disagree." Dillon leaned back his head and let out a sigh. "Okay, what's the favor, Grandad?"

"Stay with me until I pass."

For at least twenty seconds, he stared at his grandfather without blinking before letting out a choked, "What?"

Grandad waved his hand in the air like he was swatting away a fly. "Oh, it shouldn't be long. One, maybe two weeks tops."

Dillon practically stumbled back to his chair and sank back into it. He ran a shaking hand through his hair. "Why-why are you asking me to do this? I came when you called. I'm here. I've visited you. Why can't I just leave?" Even as the words were coming out of his mouth, he knew how selfish they sounded, but there they were.

Grandad's gaze softened. "Think of it as a guilt-trip or blackmail."

He didn't know whether to feel amused or angry.

"You've been away for two years. The least you could give me is two weeks."

"But—" Dillon searched his mind for an excuse even as he felt himself weakening. "Dad. Parker. They'll be down to visit you."

"Dillon, the world won't end the moment you see them."

"It may several moments later," he muttered.

Grandad continued, "Fiona and Natalie can take care of getting you in and out incognito." He raised his voice. "Right, girls?"

The two "girls" entered the room sheepishly.

"We were just trying to give you two another minute of privacy," Fiona explained, handing Dillon a root beer.

"By eavesdropping?" Even reclined in a hospital bed, Grandad managed to give them a look that used to make CEOs shake in their Italian shoes.

"We're sorry," Natalie apologized but gave Grandad a smile filled with so much affection, Dillon's grudging respect for her rose a couple notches. She nodded in his direction. "We'll take care of him."

"I haven't even promised to stay yet," Dillon mumbled.

Three sets of eyes zeroed in on him, and a sense of déjà vu filled the moment. Just like those three Americans found out his identity, these three were going to find out what he was made of.

Not much, Dillon thought with a grim set of his mouth.

"Fine. I'll stay." He quickly added, "For now."

Fiona clapped her hands together in delight. Grandad closed his eyes, seeming to sink into a nap. Natalie got down to business.

"You'll need a place to stay."

"Not the hotel."

"No, I know you're aversion to the hotel, and I'm guessing you don't have enough money to put yourself in another one."

"You guessed right."

Natalie gave a brisk nod. "Then I have a place for you."

Eden is that old-fashioned House
We dwell in every day
Without suspecting our abode
Until we drive away.

How fair on looking back, the Day
We sauntered from the Door —
Unconscious our returning,
But discover it no more.
—Emily Dickinson

CHAPTER SIX

Natalie

Natalie maneuvered her silver, four-door Sedan up the winding drive that curved through a thin forest of pine trees. Her knuckles were white from clutching the steering wheel in a death grip for the last five minutes.

Catching her bottom lip between her teeth, she tried to think up a topic of conversation that would distract her from the memories that were pouring through her like a summer rain as they drew closer to her childhood home.

She decided to go with her work approach. Give the facts.

Taking a deep breath, she launched into a speech, "The cottage you'll be staying in is a two-bedroom, one and a half bath with a living room and kitchen. It's small but cozy, and the three acres it sits on give the property more than enough breathing room."

She glanced at Dillon. He was looking straight out the front windshield, but she thought she saw a ghost of a smile flit across his face. "What?"

"Are you a realtor or something?" He cleared his throat and

pitched his voice higher. "'More than enough breathing room.'"

Her lips quirked upwards. "No, but I do watch a lot of HGTV." Loosening her grip, she tapped her fingers on the steering wheel. "I'm a journalist."

She realized her mistake when Dillon stiffened, and she could have sworn the air dropped a few degrees. "Your brother had pretty much the same reaction when we met."

"I doubt it."

When she gave him a curious glance, he explained, "Parker gets along with everybody."

"Well, I think the Sanders family doesn't warm up to those in my business right away."

They emerged from the trees, and the house came into view. "And for good reason."

Natalie steered the car up the circular drive and parked right in front of the porch.

"Welcome to Garden Cottage!" She tried to infuse as much pep into her voice as possible, but it fell flat like stale soda.

As they got out of the car, she tried to see the house through Dillon's eyes instead of through her own memory-tinted lenses.

Flat, gray stones lined the foundation of the small cottage, and similar flagstones were fashioned into four steps that led up to the wide front porch. The windows were smudged and speckled from the elements. White paint was flaking off the porch railing, shutters, and siding, giving the place a forlorn look, like a grandmother who's children hadn't come to visit in a long time.

When Natalie unlocked the front door and opened it, the familiar scent of vanilla and pine assailed her senses. Everything looked just the same as she'd left it when she had come two weeks before to check things out. A lifetime ago. For a moment, she found it difficult to breathe.

"Are you okay?" Dillon's concerned voice broke her out of her trance.

"Oh, um, yes, of course." She moved out of the doorway so he could enter. She began switching on lights so he could see the wood flooring, worn furniture, and stone fireplace decorated with a pine bough wreath and resumed her running dialogue she had begun in the car. "The previous…occupants left their furniture here." She hesitated. "Well, for now anyway. So you have a bed."

Moving to the small, open kitchen, Natalie opened the window above the sink to clear the air a bit. "Master bedroom is off the entryway." She nodded toward a closed door off the kitchen. "And that's the other bedroom, but it's off-limits. Got it?" She gazed at the door for a minute before giving herself a mental shake. "I do have one favor to ask."

Dillon wandered around the small living area. "Today seems to be "Ask Dillon a Favor Day" so ask away."

"It's nothing big. Um, this neighborhood has a neighborhood watch program thing."

She twirled a lazy Susan on the counter, hoping he wouldn't think this was too strange. But she wasn't ready to reveal the complete truth yet. She wasn't even sure she understood it all herself.

"All you have to do is keep an eye out for anyone snooping around that isn't supposed to be here. You can just call me if you see anyone trespassing and stuff on the property. Got it?" Looking back up, she froze when she saw that Dillon had picked up a small, framed picture off a side table.

"This is you, isn't it?" He brushed his gaze over the room then back at the picture. "This is your house?"

"Was." Natalie strode over, smoothly took the picture from him, and stored it in her purse. "This is where I grew up, but I haven't lived here in a long time." She set her purse on the kitchen counter.

Tapping her fingers against the leg of her pantsuit, her gaze landed on the back door.

"And here's the backyard."

As they paused on the back stoop, a look crossed Dillon's face that made Natalie pause. An almost calculated, animated expression played over his features as his gaze roamed the yard.

She only saw a flat, couple acres of half-dead grass and the oak tree that stood in the center of it. "What are you looking at?"

The expression disappeared from his face. "It's nothing." He stuffed his hands into his pockets and stepped off the stoop.

Natalie followed Dillon as he headed for the tree. They entered the wide open space beneath its canopy.

"Hope used to call this the Cathedral Tree when we were younger." When the leaves were thick in the spring and summer, it certainly was like standing in a stained glass cathedral with golden and green light pouring onto the mossy ground below.

Winter had stripped the tree of most of its foliage and left millions of acorns to be crunched under the soles of Natalie and Dillon's shoes as they walked closer to the heart of the oak.

Dillon touched the grooved bark of the tree with a seemingly tentative hand. He walked around the large trunk a couple times before popping out an unexpected question, "Why is the house called Garden Cottage?"

Natalie sniffed and tugged her coat closer to her body to ward off against the slight chill in the air. "As legend has it, my grandfather—my mom's dad—started to build this place for my grandmother, and she had an affinity for flowers."

"'Started to'?"

She stuffed her hands in her pockets and took a turn walking around the tree trunk. "Unfortunately, he never finished it. He up and left his wife and unborn child one day, never to return. My mom never spoke of it much."

"What about your grandmother?"

"Never met her. When I'd ask, my mom always used to say 'the past is the past, and the present is what should be lived in.'"

Dillon peered up into the tree's branches. "Even if something in the past defines who you are in the present?"

A question Natalie often asked herself. She gave him her only answer. "I don't know."

He glanced at her out of the corner of his eye then shifted to face the cottage. "You said your grandfather never finished it, but it looks complete to me."

"My mom bought the house years ago and had it fixed up. She then left it to me and Hope."

"Oh, your mom's gone then?" he said in a flat voice that belied emotion, but Natalie wasn't fooled.

"Yes." She absently rolled an acorn back and forth beneath the sole of her suede boot, staring unseeingly at the cottage. "She's gone."

The sound of squirrels chattering and the wind rustling dry leaves filled the space between them.

Dillon cleared his throat. "So it's called Garden Cottage because there was supposed to be a garden here?"

"Yes…and no." Natalie smashed the acorn into the dirt. "My grandparents were married here in the backyard, right beneath this tree, and my grandfather promised that they'd plant something even more beautiful than a garden of flowers in this place."

When Natalie paused, Dillon raised his eyebrows, obviously anticipating the answer she was loathe to give him.

"He told her they'd plant love, faith, and hope in their family and see them blossom into a garden more glorious than any she'd ever dreamed. So the cottage was named Garden Cottage because of what would blossom within."

Dillon squinted up at the sky. "And that didn't happen," he said softly. Statement, not a question.

"No." The word came out tainted with pain. She blinked and turned away when he looked at her. Clearing her throat, she walked with crisp steps back toward the cottage. "All that ever grew here was weeds."

Flowers — Well — if anybody
Can the ecstasy define —
Half a transport — half a trouble —
With which flowers humble men:
Anybody find the fountain
From which floods so contra flow —
I will give him all the Daisies
Which upon the hillside blow.
—Emily Dickinson

CHAPTER SEVEN

Hope

I had been covertly following the gardener all day.

You think it would be boring, watching someone garden for hours on end. But no—it was fascinating.

He tended the plants as if they were children, encouraging them to grow. The garden seemed to thrive on his voice and caring presence. Once again, I literally saw a rose unfurl its petals as he sang over it, and something deep inside me twisted. I wanted to bloom like that too.

A couple of times, I almost approached him. Right before he would spot me, I'd duck out of sight again. He said he'd enjoy my company, but why would he say that? He didn't even know me.

Tu-a-wee! Tu-a-wee!

I was crouching behind a tall group of sunflowers watching the gardener pull some particularly stubborn weeds from a patch of zinnias when I heard the bird call come from above me.

Tipping my head back, I spotted a small splash of blue amidst the frosting of pink blossoms on a nearby cherry tree.

Tu-a-wee! The bluebird cocked his head, listening.

No answering call came. "Two are we! Two are we!" he seemed to cry out, in hopes of finding a friend.

Breath caught in my chest as I waited in anxious anticipation for a bird friend to reply. None did.

After warbling for a several minutes, the cherry tree bluebird spread his wings to take flight, surely to continue his search instead of straining his voice further. As he leapt off the branch, a swift breeze caught the poor bird off-guard.

I gasped as he swerved, knocking into several limbs, before plummeting to the ground.

In two soft bounds, I was by his side. My hands hovered over the still creature but didn't touch.

The bluebird suddenly lifted his head and pulled to his feet.

My sigh of relief was cut short when he tried to lift his wings and let out a painful chirp.

"Oh, no," I breathed, noticing the bird's left wing was bent at a strange angle. "I'm sorry. I-I don't know what to do."

Gripping the skirt of my dress, I anxiously watched the bird hobble a few steps. Soft noises rose from his throat, and I realized he was still trying to sing out. A wobbly smile lifted my lips.

I knew what I needed to do.

Ever so gently, I coaxed the bird into my hands and rose to my feet. My heart was beating fast and a strange buzz hummed through my hands, yet, strangely enough, my breath was steady and calm as I walked out of my hiding place and toward the gardener.

His back was to me while he pulled a wayward strand of vines out of a blue and white hydrangea bush as I approached. I stopped a couple yards away and tried to swallow. My throat was dry.

"Sir?" I called softly. The bluebird chirped from between my palms.

The gardener slowly straightened and turned around. A gentle smile flickered across his face as he looked at me. "Hello." His voice was warm and thin laugh lines spread out from his eyes.

I opened my mouth to respond but found I had no words. This was first time I had seen him up close, and it startled me.

He looked to be maybe in his mid-thirties, but it was difficult to tell. His skin seemed older, because it was tanned and looked like it had the texture of someone who spent a lot of time outdoors. The scruff of a beard shadowed his jaw and chin. However, when he smiled, he seemed even younger than me.

But it was his eyes—his eyes—that caught my attention the most. They were so very clear, and bright, and a mixture of warm colors. It was like the ocean and mountains and sunlight rolled into one.

"I-I'm sorry for trespassing," I blurted out as the silence stretched long between us.

My heart pounded in my throat. "Earlier I was just trying to escape—the path, the darkness, the cold. Well, I mean…that sounds crazy, right?" My gaze flitted everywhere but his face before finally landing on the bluebird. "Then I was afraid to come out, you see, but then this bird…h-he—" I faltered, feeling heat rise to my cheeks.

The gardener stepped closer until he was right in front of me. He cupped his hands an inch beneath mine.

I glanced up to see a questioning look in his eyes.

"May I?" He inclined his head toward the bird.

I carefully released the bluebird to him.

Though still in obvious pain, the bird seemed to enjoy the nest of the gardener's hands. The small creature gazed at the keeper of the garden and let out a mournful chirp.

"Yes, of course I can help you," the gardener soothed. He looked up, and I caught my breath, still unnerved by his piercing gaze. "Will you follow me?"

"Yes." The word slid out with surprising ease.

His eyes softened. "Come. This way."

As I followed him down one of the narrow paths that led beside the winding stream, questions arose to the tip of my tongue. *What is this place? Who are you? Why do flowers wake up when you sing to them?* But I swallowed each one.

He spoke up so suddenly that I jumped. "This garden is very special, as you'll soon find out. Make yourself at home. The more comfortable you become here, the more you'll discover." He glanced over his shoulder and gave me a smile. "I'm the gardener, as you may have guessed."

As we approached a small group of weeping willows near the edge of the garden, he paused and pulled back long strands of leaves so I could walk through. "And," he continued as he walked behind me through the veil of green, "the flowers open because they like to hear my voice and want to see me."

I barely had time to register the strange comment and the fact that he'd vaguely answered each of my unspoken questions, when we emerged from the stand of willow trees into a clearing.

The vibrant sounds of the garden faded into stillness except for the hushed bubbling coming from a fountain nestled in the center of the copse surrounded by a rich sea of white daisies.

Made of weathered stone, the fountain was at least twenty feet around. Three tiers sat in its center, like three bird baths stacked on top of each other with the largest being at the bottom and the smallest at the top. Water flowed over the tiers and into a wide pool below, sending shimmery ripples toward the moss-encrusted, two-foot wall encasing the fountain.

The fountain had an ancient quality that dominated its surroundings. Smooth, silvered stone that held fresh water flowing into the crystal clear stream that fed the garden, bringing new life. Old yet young.

Soft grass muffled our footsteps as we headed toward a red wheelbarrow sitting to the side of the fountain. Various items poked out of the overly-stuffed wheelbarrow. Shovels, trowels, rakes, baskets, a couple of plants, and several bags of what looked like fertilizer and seeds.

Gardener—that seemed to be what he wanted to be called— sifted through the items until he pulled out several clean strips of white linen as I brushed a tentative hand over the tops of the milky flowers closest to me.

I'd always thought daisies were the most raw and honest of all flowers. Petals painted in bold, simple strokes from the center, they were fresh, happy, and unpretentious pieces of creation.

He must have noticed my longing expression, because he gestured toward the flowers. "You can pick some if you like."

Tucking a strand of hair behind my ear, I sank down onto the edge of the fountain.

"I'd almost hate to," I said softly.

"And why is that?" Gardener cradled the bluebird in one hand and began to bind its wing.

I stroked the tip of my finger up the stem of the closest daisy. "Once you pick a flower it starts to die."

"It's always dying, whether you pick it or not."

Finished with his doctoring, he kissed the top of the bird's head. Once he settled the tired creature onto a soft patch of grass to rest, he plucked a flower from the ground. "But it's always living as well. And living things are meant to be enjoyed. Especially flowers."

I received the daisy he offered me and twirled it between my fingers. The petals swirled back and forth until it looked like a seamless circle of white.

"Your turn."

Startled, I looked up. "Sir?"

Hands filled with more strips of cloth, Gardener hooked one leg beneath him and settled on the wall, facing me. "You have some wounds that need to be taken care of too."

Dropping the daisy, I curled my hands closed. "I'm fine."

He raised an eyebrow, not in a condescending fashion, but more out of curiosity.

Several beats of silence passed before I released a sigh and opened my hands to reveal the deep cuts and scratches crisscrossing the palms.

With a whisper-soft touch, Gardener traced the edge of one of the more severe wounds. "Why were you reluctant to show me?"

I swallowed, wanting to hide my hands again but forcing myself to leave them open. "It's not too bad." The words came out dry as cardboard. Even I didn't believe me.

"They still need to be cleaned. Here, place your feet in the fountain."

My gaze skittered toward the water. The surface was like clear glass only slightly distorted by the water's movement and a smattering of white flower petals that floated on top. "I'll make it dirty."

I could feel the Gardener's penetrating stare on my face but kept my eyes stubbornly on the water. It was too clean, too perfect to mess up.

"If they aren't treated soon then the wounds will fester and develop an infection."

Still...I swallowed hard, closing my hands into loose fists. Tangling my fingers into the silky folds of my dress.

After a few heavy beats of silence, he finally rose and came to stand right in front of me.

When he didn't say anything, I lifted my gaze slightly to see him offering me a few strips of white cloth like the fabric he'd used to wrap the bird's wing.

"You can use these for now," he told me.

I found no censure in his eyes, just warmth and another emotion I couldn't quite put my finger on. With a tentative hand, I received his gift and held it close to my chest. "Thank you."

Clumsily, I wrapped my hands and feet so the bandages would cover the cuts but still leave room for movement. When I was finished, he plucked the dropped daisy from the ground and held it out.

Standing, I hesitated. Disappointment settled like a stone in my stomach. But was it his disappointment in me or mine in myself?

"So," I said, gaze flicking between the offered daisy and his face, "flowers are meant to be enjoyed, huh?"

A moment of silence, slight smile, then an answer, "Yes."

I received the flower. Despite his injuries, the bluebird let out a warbling song as I began to pick more daisies.

I hide myself within my flower,
That wearing on your breast,
You, unsuspecting, wear me too —
And angels know the rest.

I hide myself within my flower,
That, fading from your vase,
You, unsuspecting, feel for me
Almost a loneliness.
—Emily Dickinson

CHAPTER EIGHT

Natalie

"You can't be serious." Natalie pinched the bridge of her nose between her thumb and forefinger. Glancing at Hope, she threw her hands in the air as she tried not to yell into her Bluetooth. "What happened to 'everything is hunky dory here, don't worry about a thing' pep talk you gave me a few days ago?"

"First off," Beth replied, "I never say 'hunky' or 'dory' unless I'm referring to Channing Tatum or that blue fish from Finding Nemo. Second, Nat, this could be the piece that will bring our magazine out of obscurity."

Beth and her big breaks. Ever since Natalie had met her teacher turned friend turned boss while taking her Intro to Journalism class at Emory University, Beth had always been striving to transform media. Her goal? People sharing their personal stories unfiltered. Truth.

Natalie admired that quality. Truth was foreign to her, but she was doing everything she could to learn the language.

Perhaps because her whole life was a closet full of skeletons, then she'd married into a family more close-lipped than she was and now she was harboring the prodigal son. Yeah, irony was her cup of tea.

Natalie glanced toward the hospital door to make sure it was closed. It was, but she still lowered her voice, "I can't leave right now. You know I have some family issues."

"At the risk of sounding cruel, it sounds like Hope is fairly stabilized right now and won't miss you for a couple days. And Hank—"

"Besides Hope and Hank." Natalie bit the tip of her tongue.

Beth paused. "Oh. That."

"Yeah…that."

"Natalie, you don't even know if your suspicions are correct. I know I always say journalists are detectives with better wordplay, but Nancy Drew you are not."

She swallowed a sigh. "I know, I know." Tapping her fingers on her leg, she stared hard at her sister's still form. Leaving her even for a few hours pricked her heart and conscience, but Fiona was around most of the time to keep an eye on things. But the other times…she couldn't just leave her alone. Not with her suspicions that—

Her thoughts were cut short when the door opened, and Dillon ducked into the room. A light bulb went off in her head. "Hey, Beth, I need to call you back."

"Oh, well—"

Distracted, Natalie clicked the off button before realizing she'd cut her friend off. Whoops.

She gave Dillon a quizzical smile. "Hey, what are you doing here?"

"Visiting Grandad. Fiona picked me up. She asked me to wait in here for a minute."

Tugging off the hood of his standard gray jacket, he ruffled the front of his hair, shaking off a few water droplets.

"Raining much?"

"Some."

"Mmm." She chewed the edge of her fingernail.

"What?" Dillon asked when he noticed her hard stare.

Oh, what the heck. She cut right to the chase. "Can I trust you?"

Wariness immediately hooded his eyes. "Why?"

Well, that was reassuring. "I need to know if I can trust you enough that if I ask you to do a job, you won't run off and abandon it."

Stuffing his hands into his pockets, he rocked back and forth on his heels, brow furrowed. "A paid job?"

Natalie refrained from rolling her eyes. Barely. "Are you saying your trustworthiness can be bought?"

Miracle of miracles, that made him crack a smile. "Maybe. What's the job? What's the pay? And how long?"

Whipping out her check book, she scribbled an amount and Dillon's name. "Since your reputation to stay in one place is far from ironclad, I'll pay you this much—" She flashed him the dollar amount. He raised his eyebrows, suitably impressed. "But I won't sign my name to this until the job is over."

"How do I know you'll actually give me the check when I finish?"

She raised an eyebrow. "Well, I guess you'll have to trust me just like I'm trusting you to watch after my sister while I'm gone for the next few days."

He stilled. "Wait, what?"

"Listen, I have a work emergency I need to attend to, and Fiona usually keeps an eye on her when I run out for a little while. But while I'm in Atlanta, I need someone who can help when Fiona can't be here."

81

He sputtered, "But-but—"

Natalie sighed, rubbing an ache in her temple. "It's weird, right?"

"Uh, yeah, a little." Dillon gestured toward the bed. "I mean, it's not like she knows someone's here. Does she need a bodyguard or something?"

She winced. "Okay, answer me one thing. Have I pushed you to answer any personal questions? Pried? Prodded?"

Locking gazes with her, a muscle in his jaw ticked. "No."

"Well, then?"

Scrubbing a hand across his jaw to smooth away tension, he gave a sharp nod. "Fine, I'll do it."

Natalie felt a slight releasing in her chest. "Great. Thank you. I'll get Fiona to give you her schedule so you'll know when to come." Feeling a bit generous, she added, "And you can borrow the rental car while I'm gone." She pointed a finger at him. "It has a tracker in it, so don't even think of using it to take off, buddy."

Before he could respond, Fiona popped her head in. "Dillon, Hank is ready to see you."

He shot her one last dubious look before leaving.

Sinking into the chair beside Hope's bed, Natalie reached for her sister's hand. "I'm sorry I have to leave, but you'll be fine." Her voice trailed to a whisper as she watched Hope's still face. "We'll both be fine."

Dillon

"So now I get to babysit a comatose patient," Dillon finished, informing his grandfather what just went down between him and Natalie. He still couldn't believe he'd agreed to do it. But he was pretty much broke, and the cash was too tempting.

"Sounds right up your alley," Grandad said.

He stopped his pacing and stared at him in disbelief.

"Don't look at me like I'm crazy, boy. And it's my turn to pick the quote. Let's do a long one." Closing his eyes in concentration, he recited, "'The quality of mercy is not strain'd/It droppeth as the gentle rain from heaven/Upon the place beneath: it is twice blest.'"

"What do you mean it sounds right up my alley?"

Grandad simply looked at him. Waiting.

Dillon glared back but wracked his brain for the next few lines he recognized from *The Merchant of Venice*, one of his grandfather's favorites of the Shakespeare canon. Hank had even convinced his wife, Betty, to go to Venice for their honeymoon so he could recite excerpts from the play while they rode in a gondola. He could quote passages from practically all of Shakespeare's works and passed the gift—or curse, depending on one's point of view—to his kids and grandkids.

Finally recalling the next bit, he spouted out the lines, "'It blesseth him that gives and him that takes/'Tis mightiest in the mightiest: it becomes/The throned monarch better than his crown'.

"'His sceptre shows the force of temporal power/The attribute to awe and majesty/Wherein doth sit the dread and fear of kings/But mercy is above this sceptred sway.'"

"'It is enthroned in the hearts of kings/It is an attribute to God himself.'" Something twisted in Dillon's gut, and he swallowed hard, sinking into the chair beside the bed, fight drained out of him.

Clearing his throat, Grandad abandoned the game for a moment. "Do you remember when you were, ah, let me see, about seven? And you found that little, baby bird that the neighbor's cat had gotten to? You cried when your mama told you there was nothing we could do about it, but after you'd mourned over that little creature, you decided you were going to protect the rest of the backyard birds from that mean old cat."

Memories flooded back. "I built a birdhouse."

"Oh, yes." Grandad laughed, turning his gaze out the window to the partly cloudy sky. "Several birdhouses. More like a bird neighborhood. You and Jacob went to the library and researched how to build those Martin houses so the cats couldn't reach their nests. I don't think I'd ever seen you so determined or happy as when you were building those homes to help those neighborhood birds." He slid him a look out of the corner of his eye. "Your father still makes sure those things are in good shape every year."

Dillon's breath stilled. "He does?"

"Yep." The older man let out a series of ragged coughs before settling back against his pillow and declaring, "You should read to her."

Startled at the sudden change in topic, Dillon leaned back in his chair. "Read to who?" It dawned on him. "Hope?" He let out a short laugh. "Why would I do that?"

A far-off look entered his grandfather's eyes, indicating he wasn't in the hospital room anymore but somewhere else with someone else. "Betty used to read aloud in bed every night before we went to sleep. She had the most calming voice of anyone I ever knew. I can't wait to hear it again." His gaze cleared and landed on Dillon. "I bet Hope would like some Shakespeare."

"You think everyone likes Shakespeare. Believe me, that's not the case."

"But you do." Grandad raised his voice like he was an Elizabethan actor in tights and feathered hat, belting out the next part of the speech, "And earthly power doth then show likest God's/ When mercy seasons justice. Therefore, Jew,/Though justice be thy plea, consider this'…" He waited with an expectant look for his grandson to finish.

Swallowing a reluctant smile, Dillon recited in a resigned voice of one who doesn't quite believe what he's saying, "'That, in the course of justice, none of us/Should see salvation: we do pray for mercy/And that same prayer doth teach us all to render/The deeds of mercy.'"

~*~

"Can you give me a ride back to the cottage?" Dillon asked.

Natalie didn't even glance up from her laptop. "Done with your visit already?"

He wandered over to the chair on the opposite side of the bed from his sister-in-law and plopped down into it. "He fell asleep." After they'd recited at least three Shakespearean sonnets and a couple excerpts from *Hamlet* and *The Tempest*.

After clicking a few things, she closed the laptop and looked up at him. "Did you talk to Fiona yet about our arrangement?"

"No, I haven't seen her since she dropped me off at Grandad's room."

Natalie stood up, stretching her neck from side to side like she was working out some kinks. "I'm going to see if I can find her real quick to fill her in and tell her I'm taking you back."

After she left, Dillon kept a steady rhythm tapping his fingers on his bouncing knee. His gaze kept veering toward Hope's face before he pulled it back again to stare out the window.

Finally letting out a frustrated breath, he leaned forward, forearms resting on his thighs with his hands hanging between his knees. "Since it seems I'm going to be visiting you on a regular basis, I may as well introduce myself. I'm Dillon."

Silence.

"Yeah, well, it's nice to meet you too." Leaning back in the chair, he propped one foot on the edge of the bed and allowed himself to truly study the young woman in front of him.

Hope was so fragile-looking. Pale and thin with a heart-shaped face that looked all too serious even as she lay unaware of her surroundings. Someone had braided her hair so it lay like a soft rope of gold and brown yarn over her shoulder, and a few freckles stood out starkly against her white skin, making her look utterly young and vulnerable.

He said aloud, "My grandfather was not so subtly trying to get me to help you today. He thought I should read to you." He quirked an eyebrow. "Have any favorite books, stories?"

The smile slipped from his face the longer he watched her breathe in and out. "I think he was also trying to convince me by comparing you to a bird I tried to help when I was younger. Except the bird was dead." He grimaced, rubbing a hand across his weary face. "Which, of course, you're not." His memory took him back to when he saw the little creature lying on the ground. "It was a bluebird."

The whir and clicks of the hospital machines pressed into the space between them as the silence stretched long. He couldn't decide if it was comfortable or suffocating.

Dropping his feet to the ground, Dillon shoved all his memories, worries, and fears aside and focused solely on the girl in front of him. "So," he gave her his most charming smile, "do you want to be friends?"

A portion of your soul has been entwined with mine.
A gentle kind of togetherness, while separately we stand.
As two trees deeply rooted in separate plots of ground,
While their topmost branches come together,
Forming a miracle of lace against the heavens.
–Janet Mills

CHAPTER NINE

Hope

I was at the edge of the garden when I heard him.

The bluebird, whom I named Dickinson, needed a makeshift nest while he recovered. Gardener had supplied a basket from his wheelbarrow but told me that the best place to find a suitable amount of twigs, moss, and long grass was at the East end of the garden.

Since he kept Dickinson cozy in his large shirt pocket while he worked, he handed me the basket and pointed to the path I should follow, saying, "Just walk until you reach the trees."

For some reason, I thought the path would end abruptly at the line of trees I had first spied when I woke up in the gazebo. It didn't.

The tangy sweet fragrance of fruit teased my nose when I

stopped at the invisible line between where the garden ended and an orchard began, path stretching before me until it curved out of sight.

Bountiful amounts of twigs, moss, and grass littered the orchard floor, but I still hesitated, twisting my bare toe into the sandy dirt of the path.

Where did it lead?

The way the trees arched overhead reminded me of the path where I had woken up. The one eventually shrouded in darkness.

Shaking off the memory with a shudder, I proceeded to grab the makings of a nest on the edges of the orchard instead of venturing in.

That's when I heard him.

"Since it seems I'm going to be visiting you on a regular basis, I may as well introduce myself."

My whole body flinched at the new voice. Whirling around, several twigs and blades of grass flew out of the basket as my heart pounded.

A few feet away, on the orchard side of the path, a boy stood leaning against a sycamore tree.

Not a boy really, but a young man. A young man with eyes as large and sad as a gray sky.

Maybe it was those eyes that kept me from turning around in fright and sprinting back to Gardener.

"I'm Dillon," he said.

Hands still shaking in surprise, I blurted out, "What are you doing here?"

He pressed his lips together as though suppressing a humorless laugh. "Yeah, well, nice to meet you too."

Pressing fingertips to my forehead, I blinked several times to make sure he wouldn't disappear. "Sorry, I just…" Wanted to poke his shoulder to see if he was real. I refrained. "…wasn't expecting anyone else to be here."

Dillon remained leaning against the tree, arms and ankles crossed, his gaze steady.

For a long moment, I stared back, watching his eyes seemingly change color like a winter storm. His first words replayed in my mind. "What do you mean you're going to be 'visiting' me on a regular basis?" Where had he come from? And where was he going when he wasn't "visiting" me?

Crouching down, he plucked a piece of grass and studied it as if it held the secrets to the universe. "My grandfather was not so subtly trying to get me to help you today."

My brow crimped. His grandfather? It couldn't be Gardener, could it? He looked too young to have a grandson, though he did seem older than his appearance. "Help me how?"

"He thought I should read to you." He raised an eyebrow. "Have any favorite books, stories?"

I couldn't help the laugh that bubbled up and spilled over. "Read to me? Why?" Though I was amused, a strange warmth curled in my belly. I really did like stories.

Still twirling the blade of grass between his fingers, he answered, "I think he was also trying to convince me by comparing you to a bird I tried to help when I was younger. Except the bird was dead." His gaze flicked over to me as he murmured in an almost apologetic fashion, "Which, of course, you're not."

My smile began to fade as I wrapped my hands tighter around the basket handle and tried not to wince as my cuts stung.

"It was a bluebird," he said softly.

I flinched in surprise. "I'm helping an injured bluebird right now. His name is Dickinson." Shrugging, I tucked a piece of hair behind my ear and tilted the basket so he could see its contents. "See? I'm building him a nest."

A strange kinship bloomed between us in that moment.

Then he stood up with a start and threw the piece of grass away from him with more force than necessary. "So, you want to be friends?"

He offered me a smile—a true smile—for the first time, though behind it his loneliness and pain were evident as if the words were scrawled across his face. I wondered if my emotions were that transparent to him.

Friends.

The word made me pause. Being friends meant something. It meant trusting. I didn't even know this guy.

But the answer was already on the tip of my tongue, waiting for me to open my mouth and be released. "Okay."

Our gazes caught and held for a second before he gave a slow nod as if in acceptance of our newfound deal. It seemed like we should shake on it or something.

Without another word, he turned on his heel and walked down the path away from me, deeper into the orchard.

"Wait!" I called out. "Where are you going?" Stepping forward, I almost followed him, but stopped right before crossing the invisible line to enter the trees.

Apprehension gripped my shoulders as Dillon disappeared around the bend and out of sight.

A strange tug-of-war pulled almost physically at my body, reminding me of my struggle at the door with the key. Just the memory of that moment caused me to take two large steps backwards.

As I brought my hand up to tuck back another strand of hair, I noticed it still had a slight shake. Clenching my fingers into a fist,

I let out a hard breath.

This was ridiculous.

I needed to talk to Gardener.

By the time I arrived back at the gazebo where I'd last seen him, my chest was heaving from sprinting back. He dropped a rake he was using and caught my arm, lowering me gently, before I collapsed on the steps.

"You alright?" he asked, laughing.

"I-I—" I needed to catch my breath.

Plopping down a couple feet away from me, Gardener dragged the basket I'd dropped toward him and began to sort through its contents. Dickinson observed with a curious tilt of his head. "This is good. It will make a fine nest."

"I saw a boy."

He hummed but didn't look up, concentrating on weaving together several strands of grass. "Ah, yes, Dillon."

I'm sure my eyes bugged out. "You knew?"

"I've known Dillon for a long time. I'm not surprised he showed up here."

Smoothing the skirt of my dress across my knees, I cleared my throat, pitching my voice lower as I asked my next question, "You aren't his…grandfather, are you?"

Amusement shone in his eyes. Leaning slightly toward me as though bestowing a great secret, he whispered, "No, I am not." He laughed when I wrinkled my nose at him. "Do I really look that old?"

I shrugged and said playfully, "Maybe."

Standing, I strode over to the wheelbarrow and pulled out the daisies I picked in the fountain clearing. "Gardener?"

"Yes?" He pressed down and molded moss in the bottom of the basket with an artist's hand.

Biting the corner of my lip, I settled back on the steps. "What is this place?"

"You could probably answer that question yourself." He began to link the twigs in a circular pattern. "It's a place set apart. A sanctuary."

"Sanctuary." The word rolled smoothly off my tongue. "It's a safe place then?"

He smiled. "Yes."

"Hmm." Studying the bouquet of daisies now lying in my lap, I began to separate them into rows. "You've known Dillon for a long time?"

"I have."

"He-he asked me to be his friend." Peeking through my lashes, I tried to judge his reaction.

Gardener bobbed his head, tying off a piece of grass. "You agreed." Statement, not a question.

I tugged a small leaf off a stem. "I did."

"Good. He needs some good friends." Pausing in his work, he stared into the distance, toward the trees. For the first time, I noted an air of sadness in his expression. "He doesn't talk to me anymore."

My brow furrowed. "Why not?"

Shaking his head, he looked over at me, his comfortable smile sliding back into place. "That's his story to tell."

Averting my gaze back to my lap, I began to twist the daisies together to form a chain. "You know what he said? His grandfather wanted him to read to me." I let out a short laugh, though I didn't quite know why. "He asked if I had any favorite stories."

"There!" Gardener showed me the finished nest. Pulling Dickinson out of his pocket, he set him in his new bed with great care.

The bluebird fluffed his feathers as he adjusted himself. I smiled when he seemed to almost sigh in delight.

"Do you?"

Startled, I glanced up at Gardener. "Do I what?

"Do you have any favorite stories?"

Twisting my lips to the side, I tied together two more stems as I thought about it.

"I like the one about Peter Pan and Wendy."

"Really?" He adjusted his position so that he was facing me, his back against one of the gazebo posts. "What's your favorite part?"

My hands paused in their work. "I-I don't know." I scrunched up my nose and stared straight ahead. "I'm not even sure why it's one of my favorites. It's kind of sad." Releasing a sigh, I resumed my task of making the daisy chain. "I think it was the part about the Lost Boys. To be lost and separated from their families for so long, then getting a family. It's just so…" My voice faded as I tried to find a word.

"You know—"

I glanced up to see a small smile on Gardener's face, an unreadable expression in his eyes.

"That's not what most people think about when reading that story."

Not knowing what to do with his reply, I continued tying daisies together. "Dillon kind of reminds me of a lost boy." A lonely, friendless boy. "How do you think he got here?"

"Do you not think he belongs here?"

Meeting Gardener's gaze, confusion pulsed through me. "Doesn't he?"

Draping an arm over a drawn-up knee, he looked out over the garden. "I'll let him know that one's your favorite." He glanced over and gave me wink. "Maybe he'll read it to you."

I narrowed my eyes at his teasing. "I thought he didn't speak to you anymore."

"Doesn't mean I stopped speaking to him."

My heart softened as I remembered the ache in Dillon's eyes. "He really is a lost boy, isn't he?" I murmured, not really expecting a response.

"What about you?" Gardener tilted his head, capturing me with his gaze. His voice grew quiet, "Are you lost?"

"Me?" Turning away from his sudden intensity, I tied off the last two stems and held up the finished circle of flowers. "Of course not. I know where I am."

"And where is that?"

I arranged the daisy crown on my head and gave him a smile. "Sanctuary."

But the calm had brought a sort of courage and hope with it.
Instead of giving way to thoughts of the worst, he actually
found
he was trying to believe in better things.
--Frances Hodgson Burnett, The Secret Garden

CHAPTER TEN

Dillon

Dillon ducked into Garden Cottage, shutting the front door behind him just as a rumble of thunder shook the walls.

Rain was coming down in buckets, pounding hard against the roof. In true Mobile fashion, Spring was struggling to make its entrance as spurts of muggy and crisp days slid between grumbling thunderstorms.

He'd just dropped Natalie off at the airport. With this weather, he wondered if her flight to Atlanta would be delayed.

Tossing his brown leather bomber jacket over the back of the couch, he rifled through his still-packed duffel bag that rested on top of the beat-up, stained coffee table.

He hadn't taken up residence in the master bedroom like Natalie suggested, opting to crash on the overly-stuffed sofa or recliner instead. One, he wasn't planning on staying long, and two, he felt like he was intruding somehow. After staying in hostels and boarding rooms the past two years, staying in someone's home felt a bit too...personal for his taste.

Dillon suspected the master belonged to Natalie and Hope's dad since their mom was out of the picture. Natalie hadn't mentioned him once, but he didn't want to ask. It would only lead to her feeling free to ask him questions.

Grabbing a full change of clothes, he closed himself in the bathroom and turned on the shower head full-force. The rain was putting him in a dark mood, and he wanted to wash it away.

Or maybe it isn't the rain at all, Dillon thought, shoving his wet hair back with both hands as the hot water pounded his face. What else could it be?

He'd already made a grudging peace with staying in Mobile for a short while. Sure, he still wanted to get the heck out of Dodge and back into Anonymity, but if that meant forsaking Grandad's last wish, then he'd never forgive himself. He already had regrets. He didn't think he could live with any more.

The longer he stayed in the shower, the more agitated he grew until finally he slammed the faucet off and stepped out of the tub, only to slip on the tile floor.

Grabbing the edges of the pedestal sink, he kept himself from going down. His heart beat thickly in his throat as he stared at his wide-eyed reflection in the mirror.

It was the first time in a long while he'd really looked at himself. As the shock faded from his eyes, other emotions appeared in their depths that made his chest tighten. Deep down, he'd harbored a secret wish that he hadn't changed that much. He was better than his conscience declared him to be.

The new hardness of his features and hopelessness in his eyes gave no such answers. Only emptiness.

Glaring at his reflection, the frustration that had been brewing beneath the surface boiled to the top, and he slammed the side of his fist against the wall beside the oval mirror.

The glass shook, the action left him tired. And he knew what was bothering him.

He was so lost.

It was strange. Some people think moments of revelation come during life-shattering events. Dillon's life had already been shattered, and he'd only been left wandering in a fog of confusion.

The quiet moments, the alone moments. Those are the times where thoughts that were being suppressed and shoved aside because there was too much clamor and noise are finally set free. Like releasing a breath that was being held too long.

Dillon had no idea what to do about this revelation. Or if he should do anything.

Maybe he deserved to be lost.

"God…" The word rolled off his tongue. It had come from somewhere deep. From a place he thought had been declared permanently silent long ago. "I need some direction."

A wish, or a prayer?

A sudden memory flashed through his mind of his first family camping trip when he was seven. His dad told him and Parker if they ever got lost in the woods to stay where they were, and he would find them.

Sure enough, Dillon had wandered off and lost his way close to nightfall. Remembering his father's advice, he'd stayed put, yelling at the top of his lungs for someone to find him.

His dad discovered him just a half an hour later, cold and hoarse. He ate five s'mores that night.

Shutting his eyes, Dillon recalled another night standing in the middle of his dad's study, his father imploring him to stay. But that time he didn't listen.

Letting out a harsh breath, he shrugged on a dark blue t-shirt and sweatpants. The rain was still assaulting the roof and windows as he headed into the kitchen to find something to eat.

Opening the freezer door, he stared blindly, his mind still fighting to release thoughts and memories he wasn't sure he was ready to face.

Grabbing a Hot Pocket, he shut the door before he got freezer burn. The pepperoni and cheese pastry was heating up in the microwave when he heard a sound like water pouring out of a faucet.

He checked both the kitchen and bathrooms before discovering the sound was coming from behind the closed door of the second bedroom, or The Forbidden Room, as Dillon dubbed it in his mind ever since Natalie's obvious hints and reluctance for him to go in there.

Wrapping his fingers around the brass doorknob, he only hesitated for a split second before opening the door and switching on the light.

Hope's room, he guessed.

Soft green walls encased the space. A white, wrought iron bed covered in a faded patchwork quilt sat against the wall across from the door with two white nightstands on either side. Glow-in-the-dark stars smattered the ceiling above the bed.

Two overly-stuffed, white bookcases flanked a spindly desk shoved beneath the one window. Water was pouring from a hole in the ceiling, creating a large puddle on the hardwood floor in front of the bookcase to the left of the window.

Running back to the kitchen, Dillon rummaged through the cabinets until he found a pail in the pantry before rushing back to the bedroom and shoving it beneath the leak, cold water sloshing over his hands. He groaned as it began to fill at a fast rate. His mind sprung into overdrive as he ran through the various possibilities to keep the rest of the floor from getting ruined.

Seventeen minutes later, the outside garbage can had been hastily wiped down and stuck beneath the small waterfall, towels soaked up a majority of the puddles, and the rain lightened considerably.

Using a hairdryer he fetched from the bathroom, he was attempting to dry the two dozen or so damp books he rescued from the bookshelf when the rain finally stopped. There were still another few dozen that still looked dry he left on the shelves.

Hope must have been some bookworm.

Amusement tipped his mouth to the side when he noticed a copy of Shakespeare's *Romeo and Juliet* among the assortment of novels, plays, and books of poetry.

"Guess Grandad was right," he murmured. Picking up the half-dry copy, he started flipping through the pages when he noticed handwriting scrawled in the margins of almost every page.

Curious, he turned to the beginning. Next to the line "A pair of star-cross'd lovers take their life," Hope had written:

Star-crossed? More like cross-eyed.

Dillon let out a snort and kept reading.

It truly is a "tale of woe" because, just like their parents, Romeo and Juliet let their emotions take over so fiercely that they couldn't see straight, and it only ended in violence and sorrow. Maybe that was Shakespeare's point? I just really don't see him writing this as an epic love story like it's viewed today, rather than a morality play. Maybe I'm a skeptic…no, that's not true. I'm a HUGE romantic. But love didn't win the day here. Cold water in the face did. And that's not fun for anyone.

He liked this girl.

For the next few hours, Dillon sat on the barstool reading through Hope's comments in several books—*The Magician's Nephew, Tom Sawyer, The Wayfarer's Inn, Divergent.*

Sometime in the middle of reading, he'd taken the Hot Pocket out of the microwave and scarfed it down.

Most of what Hope had to say was lively, interesting, thought-provoking, and sometimes amusing him to such a degree that he laughed out loud, startling him. It'd been such a long time since he heard the sound of his genuine laughter that it had become foreign to his ears.

When his head began to droop, he decided it was time to hit the sack. Before he headed for the couch, he wanted to select a book to read to Hope the next day. Grandad's idea didn't seem as ridiculous now.

Peter Pan by J. M. Barrie caught his eye. It'd been one of his favorites as a kid. Who didn't like pirates, swordfights, and flying? From the state of the worn cover and dog-eared pages, it looked like it was one of Hope's favorites too.

Setting the book aside to bring with him in the morning, Dillon stumbled over to the couch and fell across its length in exhaustion. He tugged an afghan from the armrest and pulled it up to his chin. For the first time in the few nights he'd arrived in Mobile, he felt like he might actually get some good sleep.

Second star to the right and straight on 'til morning.

My mother always says people should be able to take care of themselves,
even if they're rich and important.
--Frances Hodgson Burnett, *The Secret Garden*

CHAPTER ELEVEN

Natalie

She remembered the first time she saw Parker.

It was five months after Carol Sanders' accident involving a hit-and-run driver, and three months after the youngest Sanders' son had dropped off the face of the planet. The Sanders were completely close-lipped, not giving any details about what had happened, how they were doing, and how the investigation was going to find the other driver.

Needless to say, this drove the media into a frenzy. Rumors were rampant.

Natalie was ashamed to admit that she was one of those who was annoyed at the Golden family of America. As if she had a right to know their private business.

Perhaps that's why she'd been almost gleeful when she found out she'd been chosen from all the Journalism students at Emory to be the first person to personally interview the Sanders men. As a special nod toward Carol, both Jacob and Parker agreed to have a student write the first piece detailing what they'd been through the past five months.

She was to meet them at their private table in the dining room of the Sanders Hotel.

Parker was sitting alone when she got there, afternoon sunlight glinting off the auburn highlights in his hair and playing across his face as he read a newspaper. When he looked up at her, she was struck by the intensity of his gaze.

They exchanged strained pleasantries as they waited for Jacob with Parker explaining how he was running late because his mother was having a rough day.

For the first time, Natalie wasn't burning up with questions. In her secret heart, she'd planned to make the piece a grand expose, unlocking the skeletons in the Sanders' family closet. Instead, after Jacob arrived, they all slowly bonded over filet mignon, tiramisu, and stories of Natalie and Jacob's hometown of Mobile.

She'd struggled to hold back tears at the still-raw grief evident in the two men before her once they got around to telling their side of the story. They mainly gave facts, but their pauses and expressions revealed the deeper story to Natalie's keen eye.

Once the article was released, Parker called to thank her for being tasteful and true.

Then he asked her out for coffee.

The article had gotten international attention, and with the attention came several job offers Natalie eventually turned down in order to form her own informative online magazine with Beth. Staying in Atlanta was a plus too because of her new relationship with Parker.

Now over a year later Natalie was waiting in the Atlanta airport for Beth to pick her up, privy to her own Sanders' secret and exhausted from her delayed flight.

Adjusting the strap of her purse on her shoulder, she struggled to pull her phone out as it alerted her that she had a new text message.

TURN AROUND.

Brow furrowing, Natalie turned. A bright smile broke across her face.

Abandoning her bags, she ran forward and launched herself into Parker's waiting arms.

He chuckled against her hair as she squeezed him. "Miss me? I think I missed you a little."

She released a sigh before pulling back to receive his kiss. "You have no idea." Narrowing her eyes, she thumped him lightly across the chest. "Wait a minute. Don't you have a meeting right now?"

"Yeah, with you." Parker smoothed his thumb across her cheek. "How's Hope doing?"

Some of the energy leaked out of her smile as she remembered all she had left in Mobile. "Same." Rising on her tiptoes, she gave him another quick kiss before they headed back to fetch her bags. "Beth's at home cozy and asleep?"

"Yes, though she commanded me to tell you that she needs to meet with you tomorrow morning at nine."

Natalie groaned. "She might get lucky if I make it by ten. With coffee and bagels."

Dillon

He was on the roof.

It'd been two days since Natalie had left and Dillon had started reading to Hope. He read aloud her margin scribbles alongside the text, wondering if somehow they could bring back the girl who wrote them.

He even brought the copy of *Romeo and Juliet* to his grandfather. Grandad responded to Hope's comments Dillon read aloud as if she was in the room conversing with him.

"She's a thoughtful one, that girl," Grandad said once. "Even if she does think Romeo's fickle."

Dillon had returned to Garden Cottage that night to another rain storm and water again pouring into the garbage can in Hope's room.

Enough was enough.

The next morning, he found a ladder, some tools and supplies in the detached shed and climbed up on the roof to fix the hole.

He'd always liked working with his hands. Before he left home, he'd considered majoring in architecture or even something to do with landscaping. Even while he was abroad, he'd found odd jobs in construction. Creating something out of nothing, or fixing something broken to make it even better than before. Those were the things he gravitated toward and was naturally good at doing.

The hole wasn't too big, about the size of his hand. He was about to pound a nail with a hammer when a young voice jerked him out of his concentration.

"Chessie, come back here!"

A gray streak bounded across the yard and disappeared into the rose bushes beneath one of the barred windows. Two children, a boy and a girl, followed in quick pursuit, their short legs stumbling on overgrown patches of grass.

The girl skidded to a stop when she spotted Dillon, her dark, almond-shaped eyes expanding in surprise. Her abrupt stop caused the boy to run into her from behind, and they both sprawled onto the ground.

Dillon tossed the hammer aside and climbed down the ladder before rushing over to kneel beside them. "Hey, are you okay?"

The two kids, obviously brother and sister judging from their similar facial features, stared up at him, frozen, their mouths shaped into two perfect "O's". The brother snapped to attention first, quickly scrambling to his full height of four feet and squaring his shoulders.

"Who are you?" the little girl asked, her chin-length, silky black hair all askew.

"I'm Dillon." He offered her his hand, and she allowed him to heft her to her feet.

"And who are you?"

"Daisy, and I'm seven," she replied. She jerked a thumb over her shoulder. "And this is my brother, Mickey, he's ten. We live in the house behind you."

"Be quiet, Daisy!" The brother pulled her back roughly by the shoulders. "You know what Mom says about talking to strangers."

Dillon took a few steps away from them, towards the bushes, hoping the distance would put them at ease. Bending down, he searched through the mix of brown and green leaves until he spotted a patch of gray. "Is that your cat? Bessie?"

"Chessie," Daisy corrected, breaking away from her brother and coming to stand beside him. "It's short for Cheshire."

He cocked his head and smiled at her. "Like the Cheshire cat from *Alice in Wonderland*?"

"Yes!" she exclaimed, clapping her hands together. "Sometimes Chessie licks his lips right after he eats, and it looks like he's smiling too."

"It's creepy," Mickey grumbled. He had eased up beside them and was assessing the cat with crossed arms and a scowl.

Dillon tapped a finger against his lips. "Mickey, Daisy, and Cheshire?"

"Our parents met at Disney World," Daisy explained.

"Ah, I see."

The three of them stared into the bushes at the statue-like cat for a few moments before the sister spoke up again.

"Did the Princess come back?"

Dillon's brows pinched together, not sure he'd heard her right. "Who?"

"The Princess," Daisy stressed. "She took a shortcut through our backyard and told us she was running from an angry ogre and was late for the ball."

Mickey rolled his eyes. "It was a story, Daisy. She didn't really mean it."

The little girl slammed her hands on her hips. "Then why was she wearing a ball gown, like a princess?"

"It was just a dress," he mumbled. "And it was a long time ago. Why can't you just forget it?"

"Whoa, there," Dillon cut in, wanting to stop the argument before it went any further.

Obviously their parents' obsession with a fairy tale world made a strong impression on their daughter. But one thing Daisy had said confused him. "Why do you think I would know where the… princess is?"

She squinted up at him as if he were the village idiot. "Because she lives here."

Just then, Dillon heard a voice calling from the neighbor's house behind them, probably their mom. A spooked Chessie sprinted from the bushes back toward the kids' backyard.

Mickey groaned and followed, yelling behind him to his sister, "Come on!"

Daisy waved. "Bye! And tell us when the Princess comes back."

Watching them disappear, a strange apprehension nipped at him. He looked back at the cottage. A princess. Could she mean Hope? If that were the case, then who was the 'angry ogre'?

"Excuse me!"

Dillon's spine stiffened as he spotted a very pregnant woman waddle toward him from the direction where Daisy and Mickey had just fled. She had a kind smile that made her eyes curve like two half-moons, but he was still wary.

Talking to two kids was one thing, but an adult would be more inclined to recognize him. Why had he told the kids his name?

"Hello," the woman greeted when she was close enough to hold out her hand for him to shake.

Receiving her hand, he felt like loser for making her walk that far when he could have easily met her halfway.

"My name is Jan-di," she told him. She jerked a thumb over her shoulder toward the roof of a house in the distance. "My husband Cooper and I are your neighbors."

"I'm not your neighbor. I mean—" He tried to backpaddle. "I work for the owner. I'm just staying here awhile til the job's done." "

Jan-di shielded her eyes as she studied the roof. "You fixing up the place?"

At the moment? "Yes." No need to go into details.

"I'm glad to hear it. It's a lovely old place and deserves some sprucing up." She eyed him. "Do you paint?"

He blinked. "Paint?"

"Yes." Jan-di placed both her hands on the small of her back as though in support as she stared up at him. She was at least a foot shorter. "Our last painter had to stop mid-job because he broke his arm and fractured his neck from falling off a ladder."

That made him want to climb back on the roof right away.

"I feel awful for him, but now we're left with a primed house desperately in need of a coat of Honeysuckle Yellow paint. My husband works full-time, and I'm in no condition to do it. Plus, we're having the neighborhood barbeque at our house in a few weeks."

Dillon tried to get this straight. "Are you asking me to paint your house?"

She held up her thumb and pointer finger, almost pinching them together. "It's small. And we can pay you double the standard rate if you do a good job and get it done on time. It would really, really help us."

He ran a hand through his hair as he tried to shake off the shock of the offer. More money would be good. But what if he was recognized? Jan-di hadn't acted like she knew him, but what about her husband?

She waited with wide, expectant eyes. And she was pregnant and under stress…

Repressing a sigh, he said, "I have another job, so I'd have to work on my own schedule."

Jan-di nodded with enthusiasm. "Of course."

His shoulders slumped, and he gave her a small smile. "Okay, I'll do it."

She clapped her hands together, looking like she was about to jump into the air except for the beach ball of a stomach keeping her grounded. "Wonderful! We already have all the paint and supplies. When can you start?"

Dillon scratched the back of his neck. "Um…" He wasn't scheduled to visit Grandad and Hope until later that afternoon. "As soon as I finish patching this hole. So like, an hour?"

Her smile glowed. "Perfect. I'll set everything you need on the back porch. Just head over when you're ready." She waved a hand in the air as she waddled back home.

I have learned now that while those who speak about one's miseries usually hurt, those who keep silence hurt more.

C.S. Lewis

CHAPTER TWELVE

Natalie

Beth wasn't the most organized person in the world.

Natalie popped a bite of her honey bagel slathered with cinnamon cream cheese in her mouth and washed it down with a gulp of her latte. She needed some fortification after three days of nonstop interviews with clients, editing articles, checking up with her in-laws, and brief quality times with Parker. Like lunch time hour brief.

Not to mention, she'd arrived at eight that morning at the small office space they'd rented out for *Unfiltered Magazine* and found Beth tossing papers like a mail chute as she attempted to locate an important file she'd lost.

Forty minutes, two cleaned-out filing cabinets, one yelled at intern later and they still hadn't found it.

"I told you I needed you back," Beth said as she shoved aside a stack of papers from her desk chair and plopped down, her chin-length, blond hair askew.

Natalie's eyes crinkled in mirth over the edge of her coffee cup. "Maybe so, but I do think you were too hard on Arielle. It can't be easy working as an intern for the most disorganized person on the planet. 'Bring me a cup of coffee!' 'Sorry, boss, it got lost between copies of last year's tax returns and Starbucks receipts. Oh, is that the pizza we ordered last month?'"

"Ha, ha," Beth said dryly. "You know why I like paper copies of everything and backups of my backups. You never know when you might need them."

"True, but I don't understand why you make copies and then set them in random places. You need a professional organizer's help."

Her boss winked. "Why do you think I keep you around?"

Natalie tossed a balled-up napkin at Beth's head. It bounced off harmlessly, and she barely even blinked.

"Ms. Jones?" Arielle stood in the office doorway, shifting her feet, a manila file folder clutched in her hands.

Beth shot out of the chair. "Thank heavens! You found it!" She snatched the file from her and began flipping through its contents.

Natalie gave the girl an appreciative smile. "Thank you, Arielle. May I ask where it's been misplaced?"

She pointed over her shoulder. "It somehow fell behind the coffeemaker and slid underneath a bookshelf."

Natalie's eyebrows rose. "The bookshelf by the restroom door? That thing is heavy."

The intern shrugged. "My dad owns a furniture moving company. I've had lots of practice."

"Well," Beth shut the file with a soft thump, "I, for one, am impressed." She pointed at Natalie. "Our employees will go to no limits to get what they need and want."

"Like you going out during lunch to buy a broom and dust pan?"

"My office is not dirty, Nat, just a bit…cluttered. Yes, is there something else?"

Beth's last question was directed at Arielle, who was still hovering in the doorway.

Twisting her hands together, the girl's eyes darted between her two bosses. "Actually, yes. It's never seemed like a good time before, but—" She hesitated.

"But, what?" Natalie asked, half-distracted as she sifted through some loose papers on the desk.

"I have a story, well, information about something that could be the start of a really good story, like explosive. And it's perfect because of the personal nature of the piece—"

Beth tapped her foot. "Spit it out, Arielle."

Her words came out in a rush, "It's about Dillon Sanders."

Beth's foot paused in its tapping, and Natalie's hand froze, clutching a piece of paper in the air. She could have sworn time stopped for a full two seconds before Beth's voice came crashing back in.

"Dillon Sanders? That trail is cold. What could you have possibly found?"

"Him," Arielle said simply.

Natalie's heart began to beat double-time. She lowered her hand before they noticed the sheet trembling. Arielle's next words sounded like they were spoken through a narrow tube.

"You know how I was in Ireland last week with Marcia to research that story we're doing on Ryan O'Toole? Well, Marcia let me have a day off, so I met up with a couple friends who are studying abroad, and we ended up in this little town, Kerryglen." Her golden brown eyes became serious. "Dillon was working in a pub there."

"How can you be sure?" Beth questioned.

"I recognized him, but when my friends and I started asking questions, he got all strange. He was using a fake accent but bolted from the room when his boss called him Dillon. I did some digging around town, and apparently he'd been hiding out there a couple months."

"Nat, are you okay?"

She gave herself a mental shake and noticed Beth and Arielle staring at her with worried expressions.

Beth walked closer. "You look a bit pale."

Natalie turned to the intern and asked carefully, "Do you think he's still in this town, uh, Kerryglen?"

Arielle shook her head. "No, he left by train to Dublin, but I don't know where he went from there." She leaned forward. "But your family might have the resources to find him."

Licking her lips, Natalie stood up. "No, no. We're not even positive it was Dillon, are we? Europe's a big continent. He'd be long gone by now."

"Nat," Beth grabbed her arm before she could leave the room, "this is the first hope anyone's had in finding Dillon in two years. Don't you think you owe it to Parker to at least see where it leads?"

She yanked her arm away, immediately feeling bad at her friend's surprised then hurt expression. But she couldn't let Beth get her journalist instincts firing. Things were still too fragile. "Don't mention this to Parker. I'll-I'll bring it up when the time's right."

Beth opened her mouth as if in protest, but Natalie held up a hand to silence her.

"I think my family has enough on their plate right now without throwing speculations about the Prodigal Son into the mix." She squeezed Beth's hand and threw Arielle a smile to soften the tension. "But thank you for informing us." Picking up her purse, she headed out. "I have to meet Parker for lunch. See you two later."

Only when she was in the relative privacy of her car did she let out the shaky breath she'd been holding. Pressing her forehead against the steering wheel, she forced her hammering heart to calm down.

She could do this. It was just a small wrench, but hopefully one she dealt with for the moment. Arielle had just caught her off guard.

A groan caught in her throat. Who was she kidding? Once Beth caught wind of a good story, she was worse than a dog with a bone. Eventually, she'd be able to tell Natalie was hiding pertinent information. She might already suspect something was off.

Just a while longer, Natalie coached herself. For Grandad's sake. He and Dillon had a deal. They were getting along and didn't need journalists hounding them in the middle of it all.

She bit her bottom lip. But how long could Dillon keep his word to hang around? Especially since she promised to pay him in a couple days.

And she was essentially being dishonest with Parker. Guilty by association, right? Lying in her silence.

Art is made to disturb. Science reassures.
There is only one valuable thing in art: the thing you cannot ex-
plain.
—Georges Braque

CHAPTER THIRTEEN

Dillon

"Don't you two have schoolwork or something?" Dillon asked.

Mickey and Daisy were sitting cross-legged on their back porch watching him carefully paint around the window trim. Jan-di had informed him that she homeschooled her kids, so they'd be around almost all day unless they had extracurricular activities. She said to just say the word if they ever got underfoot.

They'd come outside ten minutes ago and hadn't said a word. Not necessarily underfoot.

But it was seriously beginning to creep him out.

"It's our lunchtime," Daisy replied.

"Well," he wiped some moisture from his forehead with the back of his wrist, "aren't you going to eat?"

"We're fast eaters." She laid down on her stomach and began swinging her legs back and forth in the air, almost nailing her brother in the nose. He shoved at her foot in disgust, and she

121

scooted away without comment. "Do you always paint houses?"

"Not always."

"What do you do?"

"Just stuff."

"That's not an answer."

"Yes, it is."

Daisy wrinkled her nose. "Not a good one."

He lifted his eyes heavenward, trying not to smile. "What would be a good answer then?"

"Hmm, well, our daddy is a doctor. That's something."

"That is..." Dillon concentrated on swiping the tip of his paintbrush around the bottom corner of the window frame. "...something."

"Do you have any family?"

He almost dropped the brush. Okay, that was enough questions for today. "Isn't your lunch break over?"

"Not for another..." Daisy checked her Little Mermaid watch, her brow furrowed in concentration. "Um..."

Mickey rolled his eyes and grabbed her wrist to take look for himself. "Twenty-three minutes."

Great. Distraction time.

"Hey, do you guys want to help me paint?"

"Yes!" Daisy exclaimed, jumping to her feet as if this was what she'd been waiting to do her whole life.

Mickey stood too but with much less vigor.

"Here." He handed Mickey a small paint roller. "You dip the roller in the paint, like this, and then you choose a board and go side to side. Not up and down." He demonstrated before handing the roller to Daisy. "Got it?"

"Side to side," Mickey repeated, executing the job efficiently. "Like on The Karate Kid."

"Right. Good movie."

"Second one's better." The tip of Mickey's tongue protruded from the corner of his mouth as he concentrated on making every stroke perfect. His sister followed suit, dripping a lot more paint on the tarp.

After watching them for a minute, Dillon picked up his paintbrush, and they all worked in silence until Jan-di popped onto the porch.

"My, my, what do we have here?" she asked, her eyes sparkling in surprised delight.

Dillon glanced at his watch, startled to see almost an hour had passed. "Sorry I kept them out here for so long."

"No, it's fine." Placing a hand on Daisy's shoulder, she gestured at the half-painted back wall. "It's looking wonderful."

"Mommy," Daisy said, bouncing on her toes. "Mickey and I painted the whole bottom of the wall!"

Jan-di raised her eyebrows, looking genuinely impressed. "Really?"

Mickey nodded, his face flushed from working. "Dillon showed us how to do it right."

"It's true, they did." Dillon eyed their work. A strange rush of pride surged through his chest. "You can dock it from my pay."

"Of course not!" The woman seemed almost offended. "I can work it into their curriculum. Count it as Home Ec or P.E. or even Art. Beautiful job, each of you!" She planted big kisses on each of her children's heads.

Mickey shied away. Daisy grinned.

Jan-di looked at Dillon, tipping her head to the side. "Would you like to take a break? Have something to drink?"

"Thanks, but I brought something." He gestured to his half-filled water bottle sitting on the ground.

"Well, let me know if you need anything. I'll get the kids out of your way."

Mickey and Daisy began to plead and whine to stay. Dillon started to speak up and say it was fine if they wanted to hang out with him. He'd gotten used to their company. But he didn't, and Jan-di herded the children inside with a firm but gentle hand.

Since he wasn't scheduled to visit Grandad and Hope until later that night, Dillon worked through most of the afternoon and left Jan-di's place shortly before suppertime, hoping to catch a shower before heading to the nursing home.

He cut back to the cottage through a gap in the privacy fencing, breathing in the heady scent of honeysuckles growing in abundance around the edges of the yard.

Jan-di had told him the honeysuckles had inspired the paint she chose for her house. Warm, golden yellow with creamy white trim. She said the colors made her happy.

He shook his head with a smirk as he remembered briefly meeting her husband, Cooper, who'd informed him that Jan-di was in her "nesting" mode, whatever that meant. Something to do with making the home perfect for the baby when it came.

In Dillon's opinion, the house, except for the lack of paint, was already as close to perfect as it could be, as was the happy family inside. It almost hurt to be around.

After taking a quick shower and changing out of his paint-splattered clothes, there was a little while before he had to leave. To kill some time, he decided to reshelf the books that were still lying on the kitchen counter from the other night.

The hole in the ceiling was patched up, the garbage can had been moved to its rightful place outside, and everything was blessedly dry. As he worked, he eyed a few of the other books he hadn't removed from the shelves.

He'd read Hope most of *Peter Pan,* and they only had a couple chapters left. Natalie still hadn't given him a definitive date for her return, so he might as well find another book to start. If he didn't finish by the time Nat got back, she could continue reading it to her sister.

Thumbing over a few titles, he tried to pry out a copy of *The Borrowers,* but the books were wedged so tightly together that when he gave it a hard tug, the book next to it popped out and tumbled to the floor, a piece of folded paper fluttering from its pages.

Reaching down, he picked up the book—*The Secret Garden*—before retrieving the fallen sheet of paper and unfolding it.

A colorful sketch of a garden done in pastels greeted him. Nestled within the riot of flowers was a simple gazebo. Though not particularly skillful, thoughtfulness was in every line drawn on the page. The words "My Secret Garden" were written in loopy, cursive letters in one corner.

As if pulled by a magnet, Dillon turned back toward the window to view the blank canvas of a backyard and held up the drawing next to it. Ideas popped up out of the fallow ground in his mind like spring bulbs.

In his mind's eye, patterns sketched themselves across the ground, finally ending in an imaginary blueprint of a gazebo slightly different from the one in the drawing. A structure that would incorporate the grand, old Oak.

Try as he might, he couldn't erase the image or the bubble of excitement that threatened to break the surface. Garden Cottage was always meant to have a garden.

"I'm not going to be here long enough to finish it anyway," he mumbled, forcefully pulling away from the window and plopping down on the bed.

Laying on his back, he held the picture above him. A dream cast onto paper. It'd been a long time since he'd buried his own dreams of building and creating places for people to enjoy and declared them dead. Apparently he'd buried them alive, and they were fighting to break the surface.

Letting out a frustrated grunt, he wedged the sketch back within pages of *The Secret Garden* and tossed the book on the bed beside him. At least that's what he meant to do.

Instead, he threw the paperback with more force than necessary, and it smashed into a framed picture on the nightstand, toppling it to the floor with a small crash.

Dillon's eyes weighted shut for a second before fluttering open to view the lifeless glow-in-the-dark stars on the ceiling.

Was making a mess his gift?

Shoving off the bed, he knelt on the floor by the small picture frame. It lay face-down in a misshapen circle of shattered glass. Being careful not to cut his fingers, he gently picked up the picture and turned it over.

Two girls smiled up at him. Wide, cheesy grins that caused Dillon's chest to experience an unexpected ache.

The oldest girl, who looked to be in her early teens, was obviously Natalie with her puppy dog eyes and dark hair. She had her arm slung around the shoulders of the other girl, who looked maybe to be eight or nine. They were tucked close as if trying to fill the entire picture frame and wore daisy crowns in their hair.

Dillon stared into the wide open eyes of the younger girl. They were hazel and sparkling with mischief.

Hope.

The face of the pale, silent young woman lying in the hospital bed flitted through his mind, contrasting sharply with the picture in front of him of a girl with flushed cheeks and bright gaze, like she had been running or laughing.

His breath hitched as the dreams he had in Ireland and his first night back in Mobile returned with such sudden clarity that he almost let the picture fall to the ground again. As it was, he barely made it to the bed before he sank down, his gaze glued to the face of the young Hope.

Sparkling, hazel eyes. Heart-melting smile.

Same as the girl in his dream.

His hands began to shake so hard he set down the picture and balled them into fists.

Don't freak out, he reprimanded himself. You're just imagining things because you're so tired.

That's it. He was probably still jet-lagged, right? Lots of stress. He must be hallucinating, not remembering correctly.

He rested his arms on his legs and gouged his fingers through his hair, then froze.

Then how had he known Hope had hazel eyes before he saw the picture?

Chills raced up and down his spine, and he grabbed the photo again, staring hard at the impossibly familiar little girl.

Oh, yeah, he was freaking out big time.

Freeing the picture from the frame, he stuffed it in his back pocket before leaving the room and striding out the back door, grabbing the car keys on his way.

I never hear the word "escape"
Without a quicker blood,
A sudden expectation,
A flying attitude.

I never hear of prisons broad
By soldiers battered down,
But I tug childish at my bars,—
Only to fail again!
—Emily Dickinson

CHAPTER FOURTEEN

Dillon

When he arrived at the nursing home, Dillon briefly realized three things: he'd left his phone back at Garden Cottage, he was an hour early, and people were staring at him as he breezed past on his way to the third floor. He also realized he didn't really care.

Stepping off the elevator, the bubbling of the hallway fountain followed in his wake as he jogged down the corridor and barged into Hope's room, shutting the door behind him with a firm hand.

Heart thumping at a rapid clip, he stared at the quiet girl in the hospital bed. After his mad rush, he was strangely reluctant to draw near. With a clench of his jaw, he forced himself to walk forward until he towered over her.

Dillon pulled out the picture of young Hope and Natalie from his pocket and compared the little girl in his dream to the older version. While obviously similar, the present Hope seemed to have been drained of life. Like she had buried herself deep somewhere and only her body remained in the bed—silent. No laughter.

This was wrong. She shouldn't be lying so still, seeming lost to the world.

Inexplicably, something about her pulled at him. Like she was calling out in her silence.

He gripped the picture tightly at his side, his brow furrowed deep. "Where are you?" he whispered. *Where are you?*

A strange wave of protectiveness surged through his defenses, causing his chest to tighten.

He desperately wanted to help her.

Caught off-guard, Dillon stumbled back a few steps. Scrubbed his hands over his face, through his hair, tried to steady his breathing.

Yeah, he was going mad. Completely, over-the-top mad.

When the door opened, he whirled around in defense.

Natalie entered. Her eyes widened when she saw him, and she quickly closed the door. "Dillon," she said in a hushed voice. "What are you doing here? I thought you weren't supposed to come for another hour."

His stance relaxed, though he could still feel tension in his shoulders. "I came early."

He slipped the picture back into his pocket, not ready to discuss it with anyone yet. Maybe never. "Why didn't you tell me you were coming back?"

"You didn't get my texts?" she asked, her voice still lowered.

"No. I mean, I don't think so. I've been busy all day and haven't had much time to check my phone. Why are you whispering?"

"I, oh, sorry." Her voice returned to normal. "I just didn't want anyone to hear, I guess." Avoiding his gaze, she seemed to contemplate saying something, casting a glance at the door before walking over to her sister. "Fiona says you've been taking good care of her."

His eyes narrowed. Something was off, but he couldn't put his finger on it. He pushed the feeling aside as he watched Natalie smooth Hope's hair with a slight sinking feeling in his stomach. "So," he cleared his throat.

She looked at him expectantly. "Yes?"

He shuffled his feet slightly. "I guess you won't need me to keep her company now that you're back."

Her eyes widened. "You can if you want to. It helps to know other family's here when I can't be."

Family.

Before Dillon could respond, the door creaked open again.

"Hey, Nat, did you—" The person in the doorway froze in the middle of loosening his tie with one hand and fisting a fast food bag in the other.

Dillon felt the air crash out of him like a roaring waterfall. No. He wasn't ready. Not yet. Not yet.

Parker

Dillon.

Parker's body was as immoveable as a two-ton brass statue.

"Dillon," his voice croaked out, still unsure if he was seeing correctly.

His brother, his long-lost kid brother, looked just as spooked as Parker felt. "Hey."

"Hey," he repeated, drawing out the word. His statue-like stiffness began to melt.

"'Hey'?" The paper bag from Wendy's crumpled in his hand. "Is-is that all you have to say?"

Dillon's gray-blue gaze, a true mix of their mother and father, seemed to study him with a wary expression. A muscle in his jaw jumped. He looked like he was about to bolt straight out the window.

Parker wasn't sure whether to open it for him or not. "Where have you been?"

"Overseas."

"Overseas, where?"

"Europe."

"For how long?"

"All two and a half years."

"Finally!" Parker exclaimed, causing Nat and Dillon to flinch. "An answer that wasn't just one-syllable."

He kept his stance in the doorway, afraid his brother would run if he moved one inch, and flicked a glance at his wife. "How long have you known he was here?"

She fiddled with the hem of her shirt but didn't look away. "He arrived a couple days before I returned to Atlanta."

"A week?" Parker dragged his hand through hair, a habit he'd been trying to break for years.

Nat came up and squeezed his arm. He felt the frustration try to melt away under her gentle touch, but he fought it. He couldn't believe she hadn't told him. "Why didn't you tell me?"

"She probably wanted me to right away," Dillon spoke up. "But she tricked me into working for her instead." He gave her a rueful grin that didn't quite reach his eyes. "Though this wasn't part of our deal."

Parker frowned. "Deal? What deal?"

Nat threaded her arm through his and dragged him out of the doorway, closer to his brother. He stiffened, but didn't pull away. "Dillon needed a place to stay and some extra cash." Her voice shook as she babbled on. "He's staying in Garden Cottage and kept an eye on Hope for me while I was gone. He's up here anyway visiting Grandad. That's why he's here."

His gaze zeroed back in on his brother. "Grandad knows?"

Dillon shrugged. "He's the one who got Fiona to contact me

about his condition."

"And Fiona—" He drew in a deep breath through his nose to keep from exploding and lowered his voice. But that didn't keep the anger from oozing through anyway. "Who else is in on the secret? The entire Gulf Coast? I'm surprised I didn't hear you were back from the newspapers." He swept a hand across the space in front of him as if envisioning the headline. "'The Prodigal Son Returns.' Has a nice ring to it, don't you think?"

"I'm not staying for good, Parker."

He let out a hard laugh. "Of course you're not. Why are you even here now? For Grandad? Why stay for him when you left Mom?"

"Parker," Natalie warned softly.

An emotion flashed across Dillon's face, brief but strong. Parker felt it like a fist in his gut. "I had to leave after what happened to Mom."

Confusion swirled inside him, mixing with his frustration. "What do you mean you 'had to'? You wanted to get away, I get that—"

"No! Yes—I mean—" He groaned, bowing his head a moment. "You don't get it Parker." He met his gaze, expression closed off. "Just keep on hating me for leaving. It's easier that way."

Before Parker could even think, Dillon had brushed passed him and was out the door.

Nat tugged on his arm. "Aren't you going after him?"

He slowly shook his head, his body going numb. "I know where he's staying." Carefully extracting himself from Nat's grip, he ended up crumpling the fast food bag even more. He asked again, "Why didn't you tell me?"

Explanations seemed written all over her face, but when she opened her mouth nothing came out.

Parker simply stared at her, too overwhelmed to even argue. "I need some time to think."

Alarm shone like two beacons in her eyes. "Parker—"

"No." He shook his head. "I can't—right now." Turning his back to her, he closed his eyes briefly. "I'm sleeping in my parents' suite at the hotel tonight." Before she could defend herself, he strode out of the room.

On the elevator ride back down to the lobby, he collapsed against the wall, hands covering his face. He was the one that was always responsible, always knew what to do. The one who always kept it together.

He drew in a shaky breath. Parker had always prided himself on being able to read people easily, especially his brother. Dillon was the more introverted of the two brothers, but Parker had always been able to read his expressions as if he were wearing a sign on his forehead that said 'happy' or 'confused.' This new Dillon might as well have been wearing signs written in another language.

But somehow, he was able to decipher two things.

One, his brother was hiding something.

Two, Parker had to find a way to tell his dad the prodigal son had returned.

Not all those who wander are lost.
J.R.R. Tolkien, *The Fellowship of the Ring*

CHAPTER FIFTEEN

Hope

Dillon came back.

He came at odd times. Sometimes I'd be waiting at the edge of the orchard, and he'd appear from behind one of the trees or would walk up the orchard path, stopping just short of coming into the garden.

Other times, I'd be at the gazebo keeping Dickinson company or helping tend flowers when Gardener would suddenly announce, "Dillon's here for a visit."

How he knew Dillon was at the orchard path even when we were clear on the other side of the garden, I never questioned. I simply set aside what I was doing and went for a visit.

He brought a copy of *Peter Pan* to read aloud. Gardener must have somehow given him the message.

I would lean back amongst the sweet flowers as butterflies flitted through my hair and listen to Dillon read about flying, imaginary lands, and children discovering what it means to be young and to grow up. Often I'd quote some of the lines along with him. I really enjoyed those times.

But today he hadn't come.

"Where is he?" I asked Dickinson. The bluebird sat nestled in his basket-nest beside me, flapping his good wing.

"Why don't you try to find him?"

Leaning my head back, I found Gardener standing above me, hands on his waist.

"Find him," I repeated. Returning my gaze to the shadowed trees, a mixture of curiosity and dread swirled my stomach. "You mean go in there?"

Gardener walked over to where the garden path ended and the orchard path began.

"Why not?"

Scrambling to my feet, I brushed off the back of my dress as I sputtered, "Well—I-I've never gone into the orchard before."

He raised an eyebrow. Even to my ears it sounded like a weak excuse.

Gardener's eyes began to twinkle, and he practically bounced on the balls of his feet. "So do you want to?"

I don't think I'd ever seen him this excited. Picking up Dickinson's basket, I held the handle close to my chest as I gulped. I'm sure my eyes looked as wide as saucers.

Did I want to? No...and yes.

Without waiting for me to respond, Gardener entered the trees and held out his hand.

His voice softened. "Come with me to find Dillon."

After casting a glance over my shoulder at the colorful garden and the gazebo in the distance, I took three tiny steps forward and placed my hand in his, squeezing my eyes shut.

He gave a gentle tug, and I stumbled into the orchard.

Immediately, Dickinson let out a sweet warble and at least a dozen birds called out, sounding like bells and wind chimes.

Cracking open one eye then the other, I relaxed my shoulders, feeling foolish for being so jumpy. Gardener wouldn't lead me somewhere dangerous like the first path, right?

He pulled me deeper into the trees.

While the garden trembled with energy and newness, the orchard's atmosphere was more reserved, except for the playful breeze winding through the tops of the tree branches, softly rustling the leaves.

The air was fresh and thick, like the earth after the spring rain, fragranced with the sweet scent of ripening fruit. Smooth grass blades tickled my toes.

I gripped the woven basket, and my bandages caught on some rough parts of the handle. I carefully pulled them loose. "What do we do now?"

Gardener swiveled around, walking backwards as he talked. I was surprised he didn't run into a tree. "We're going to find some fruit." The almost giddy smile on his face made me want to laugh out loud.

I relaxed further. "What's so exciting about fruit? And what about Dillon?"

He winked. "You'll know when you taste it. The fruit here is especially good." He turned back around to match my gait. "We can look for Dillon while we pick some. I know he's here somewhere."

I let out a breath. "Okay, let's go."

Each tree held something different than the last, and the Gardener gladly told me about each one without me even asking. We discovered many fruit trees: apple, pear, cherry, fig, and some I didn't even recognize, but we didn't find fruit ripened to perfection until we reached a peach tree.

Gardener picked one of the peaches, colored in the shades of a sunset, and handed it to me. I bit into it and sweet, sugary juice flowed over my tongue, bursting with flavor. Fresh energy surged through my body, blasting away the last of my nerves.

My eyes widened. "Wow, that is good."

He plucked another peach and rubbed the fuzzy exterior with

his thumb. "You've wondered at the things that grow here."

I nodded and swallowed my second bite quickly, giving him my rapt attention.

"All living things in the garden respond to those within it. Me, you—"

"Dillon," I finished softly.

"Yes, but there is one thing you should know." He placed the peach in the basket beside Dickinson, his deep gaze capturing my own. "The garden doesn't always produce what you want but what you need."

My brow furrowed as I processed his words. "But...couldn't what I need become something that I want?"

Gardener pulled back, his expression unreadable. "If you let it."

Not every tree was a fruit tree. There were towering pines, rich cedars, beautiful magnolias with creamy blossoms, and so many more that I hadn't even heard of. But my favorite we found was the oak tree.

I don't know why I was drawn to it. Maybe because of the sheer grandness of its shading branches that twisted up and outwards like a magic tree in a fairytale. Perhaps because it seemed like a kindly grandfather next to the small peach and apple trees that surrounded it. Or it might have been because it looked like a glorious tree to climb.

"Can I climb it?" I asked Gardener, gazing at the oak with wide eyes.

"Can you?" Teasing edged his voice.

I grinned up at him as I handed over Dickinson's basket. "Just watch me!"

In fifteen seconds flat, I'd tied my skirt in a knot so it wouldn't get in my way and ascended the lowest branch.

Gardener whistled and clapped to urge me on as I went up two more levels before stopping to catch my breath.

I drank in the view of softly rolling orchard hills and a splash of color in the distance I recognized as the garden while I straddled the branch and settled my back against the trunk.

My heart pumped warmth through my body and my hands shook a little from adrenaline. It felt wonderful.

Closing my eyes, I smiled as the breeze caressed strands of hair back from my face.

"Where are you?"

I jerked, almost toppling off the branch. "Gardener?"

"Where are you?" The whispering voice seemed to ride on the breeze, wrapping around me, and I recognized it.

"Dillon," I whispered. Sitting up straighter, my fingernails dug into the branch as I peered through the nearby trees. A few yards off I spotted a glimpse of someone running through the orchard before disappearing again.

"Did you hear that?" I called below.

"Hear what?" Gardener asked.

Much slower than I ascended, I climbed down with shaking legs. Right before I jumped down from the final limb, the whisper returned, fainter this time, *"Where are you?"*

With a gasp, I slipped and fell back, but Gardener caught and steadied me on my feet.

"Dillon." I whirled around in a circle. "I heard him call out, and I think I saw him."

Gardener grasped my shoulders, causing me to still. "Where?"

I twisted my hands into my skirt. "I-I thought I saw someone running through the trees that way." I pointed and noticed my fingers trembling.

He reached out and latched our hands together. "Will you show me?"

Gripping his hand tightly, I nodded, leading him in the general direction I thought I saw the person run. Deeper into the orchard.

The trees grew dense alongside the path, causing the shadows to congregate closer together, black and thick. Warm, wet air painted my skin in the confined space, sticking my hair to the sides of my face and the back of my neck. The path narrowed.

Muscles in my shoulders and abdomen curled tight with tension while my arms and legs trembled. I let out a gasp as a new tremor shook me. "Why am I like this?"

Gardener stopped in the middle of the path and tilted my chin up, his lips set in a firm line. "You're afraid."

I let out a choking sound. "I know."

He refused to let me look away. "But are you ready to tell me why?"

Licking my dry lips, my chin trembled in his grasp. Trying not to whimper, I forced out, "I want to go back to the garden."

His brow lowered. "What about Dillon?"

Shame filled me. How had I forgotten about him? I cast my gaze to the side and sucked in a sharp breath. "Gardener, look!"

Fog.

Strands of silver mist curled around us in a tangling mass.

I grasped Gardener's arm, my head swiveling left and right. How had it gathered at so fast? The path was disappearing from sight at a rapid speed. "How do we get out of here?" My voice muffled in the thickening air.

Cocking his head, he held up a hand as though telling me to wait and listen.

"I deserve this."

I jumped. It sounded like Dillon's voice was just a few yards away. "Dillon!" I called out. "We're over here!"

Instead of waiting for him to find us, Gardener sprinted straight into the wall of fog, dragging me along with him. When he came to an abrupt stop, I had to catch my balance before I spotted him.

Dillon stood with his back toward us, staring into the thick mass before him. He must have heard our approach, because he glanced over his shoulder.

Silver and white strands twirled between us, partially obstructing him from our sight. I could see him squint through the wet mess like he couldn't quite see us.

Relieved to see him, I started to wave and call out when his head snapped back around and he flinched as though surprised. He reached out an arm as though beseeching someone before him. *"No!"*

The desperation and grief uttered in that one word made my breath catch. Releasing Gardener's arm, I hurried toward Dillon, batting away wisps of fog trying to blind me. Right before I was close enough to reach out and touch his shoulder, he ran forward into the mist, disappearing from sight.

I started to follow, but after a few steps I stopped and looked around helplessly.

He was gone.

We come from the earth, we return to the earth, and in between we garden.
–Author Unknown

CHAPTER SIXTEEN

Dillon

The rumble of the car's engine grew louder. Closer.

His arms were spread wide in surrender.

But this dream was different.

He was surrounded by fog.

Instead of the little girl running into the middle of the road, a man appeared. An old man wearing a faded plaid shirt and a fedora.

Grandad, Dillon mouthed, his chest aching. "I'm sorry."

Deep compassion radiated from his grandfather's eyes. "Don't be afraid. It's time to stop hiding."

Dillon's arms shook as he struggled to keep them spread wide. "You don't understand." The headlights were shining brighter now, bouncing off the wall of fog and scattering light fragments in the air. "I deserve this."

Grandad didn't seem to hear him as he cocked his head, a soft smile on his lips. "Do you hear that?"

Dillon listened. It sounded like someone calling his name. A girl's voice.

Glancing over his shoulder, he saw two silhouettes a short distance away. The mist parted slightly, and he thought he caught a glimpse of a girl's smiling face.

Hope.

His heart raced. But she wasn't a little girl, she was older.

Awake. As she should be.

"My boy."

He snapped his head back around.

His grandfather tugged on the brim of his fedora and sent him a wink. "Go home."

Dillon blinked, and Grandad was gone. "No!" His chest heaved.

He ran forward just as the car burst out of the fog.

Everything went white.

Dillon jerked awake, almost falling out of the recliner. His gaze flailed around until he realized he was inside Garden Cottage, and the sun was just beginning to rise.

Cold sweat covered his body, like the fog had followed him out of his dream by clinging to his skin.

Shivering, he pushed down the footrest on the recliner and stood up on trembling legs. Why had that dream affected him to such a degree? And why did he keep having these same, vivid dreams in the first place?

He swiped a hand through his damp hair and cringed. He needed a shower.

Shuffling into the kitchen, Dillon poured himself a glass of water and gulped it down before pouring himself another one. His throat was parched. He must have been yelling in his sleep.

What was the use worrying about strange dreams? His reality was screwed up enough.

Parker knew he had returned which meant Dad probably knew he was back too. He was surprised his brother hadn't come to Garden Cottage the night before and dragged him back into his "rightful" place in the Sanders empire. He was dutiful like that.

The bucket load of water he'd just swallowed threatened to come up at the thought of standing on a public platform and explaining why he'd been gone the past couple years. Facing Dad was an even worse idea, and seeing Mom again...out of the question.

Setting his glass in the sink, Dillon reached for his phone he'd been charging on the counter and noticed Natalie had left at least ten text messages and five voicemails since last night. The most recent text was sent just ten minutes before, right around the time he'd woken up.

CALL ME. RIGHT NOW. IT'S IMPORTANT.

If she was desperate to talk with him, why hadn't she just driven over?

Punching in her number, he waited for her to answer. She picked up after the first ring. "Hey, Natalie."

"Why haven't you been ans—"

"I don't think it's a good idea for me to come up there today since, you know—"

"Listen—"

"I know I promised Grandad, but maybe I could call him—" Yeah, he was a coward. "—or something—"

"Dillon!" Natalie practically screeched into speaker then immediately lowered her voice as if other people were nearby. "Stop talking, and just listen."

He tensed. Were his parents in town already?

The line crackled like Natalie had let out a long breath. When she finally spoke again, her voice was notably subdued. "I'm sorry I have to tell you this way. I wish—" Her voice cracked. "I wish I could tell you in person, but I'm helping Parker with the preparations. Wait, no, sorry, I need to tell you properly."

The dream assaulted him with vengeance. "Grandad's dead." Bile rose in the back of his throat, his eyes burned.

Natalie whispered, "Yes. Just before sunrise."

He sagged against the counter, pressing his hand over his eyes. He hadn't even visited him yesterday. God forgive him, he'd broken one promise he'd meant to keep.

"Dillon—"

He hung up.

Parker

A hollow thunk echoed through the still cemetery as the clump of dirt hit Grandad's coffin.

Parker pulled back to stand next to his father, folding his hands in front of him as he silently watched the gravediggers shovel the rest of the dirt into the hole.

On the outside, he was calm and collected, the perfect image of the faithful, dutiful son. Inside, his thoughts were racing a mile a minute.

He discreetly glanced toward where their cars were parked, but he saw nothing except for the limo and a few other luxury cars belonging to his uncles, aunts, and cousins. Jacob wanted just the family by the graveside after the funeral, and then they'd meet everyone else at the hotel for a reception.

Even paparazzi had been respectful, keeping their distance which was also helped by tight security. The rest of the family started to trickle back to their cars, so it was just him, his father, and Natalie.

Dillon hadn't come.

It was no secret that out of all of them Dillon had always been closest with Grandad, and even now, after the news had spread across the globe that Hank Sanders—America's most beloved businessman and family man—had died, his favorite grandson had failed to show up.

Parker shifted his feet the slightest bit and felt a muscle in his jaw twitch. He shouldn't have been surprised. In fact, he should be glad Dillon hadn't come. All of the attention would have shifted to him rather than the real focus of honoring their grandfather's life and legacy.

And what legacy was it exactly? Sure, his business was secure and thriving in his son and grandson's capable hands. Jacob's love of the hotel franchise with all the hospitality and people-oriented business it entailed had been passed down to his eldest son, and Parker thrived in his work.

But no matter how good a face his father tried to put on, their family was a mess.

Old memories from before his mom's accident and Dillon left, combined with his grief over his grandfather's passing and the situation with Hope were practically suffocating him. If he wasn't relieved of one of these burdens soon, he knew he was going to break.

For one brief second, Parker thought he understood why his brother had run away.

Natalie's cool hand slipped over one of his and tugged it loose from the tight grasp. Weaving their fingers together, she gave a gentle squeeze.

Immediately, his shoulders relaxed, and he let out a breath he didn't realize he'd been holding. But he didn't look at her. He couldn't after she'd kept away information of such importance from him. Why did she feel more loyal to Dillon than to her own husband?

Of course, he hadn't told his dad about Dillon being back, though he fully intended to when the time was right. Ms. Fi called a few hours after he got to the hotel the night before, telling him Grandad had taken a turn for the worst. He contacted his parents, who immediately flew down. There hadn't been a good time to bring up his brother.

"It's about time we head to the hotel," Parker finally said after several long minutes. He drew his hand away from Natalie's, feeling like he was tearing off his own hand, and turned to go. Then stopped short when he noticed his father.

The patriarch of the Sanders family always stood tall, but today his shoulders were slumped. His eyes were devoid of tears but were filled with such an ache that Parker felt like his throat was caught in a stranglehold.

He placed a hand on his arm. "Dad," he said softly.

Jacob straightened and tore his gaze away from his father's grave. "Yes." He cleared his throat. "We should go." He clamped a hand on Parker's shoulder.

As he looked into his father's eyes, he all of the sudden wanted to crumble into his arms like he had when he was boy. He wanted to forget the last two and a half years and all the animosity he'd hidden deep inside toward his brother. He desperately wanted to tell his dad everything would be fine. They'd be fine.

But he couldn't.

The words stuck in his throat, and the moment was gone.

In sooth I know not why I am so sad.
It wearies me, you say it wearies you;
But how I caught it, found it, or came by it,
What stuff 'tis made of, whereof it is born,
I am to learn...
William Shakespeare, *The Merchant of Venice*

CHAPTER SEVENTEEN

Dillon

He was going crazy. He knew he was. For two whole days, Dillon had been working like a maniac.

Most of his time was spent finishing Jan-di and Cooper's house. Jan-di must have sensed his dark mood, because she kept the kids out of his way though they begged to help him. When he wasn't working at the neighbor's, he found odd jobs around Garden Cottage. He'd already scraped the dirt and paint speckles from the windows and hosed them down as well as hammering all loose boards he could find.

When it got too dark to do any outdoor work, he even resorted to filling in any holes that speckled the walls from pictures being moved about. Not to mention he mopped the kitchen floor, repapered the kitchen cabinets, vacuumed the furniture, and cleaned both bathrooms. He didn't need sleep anyway.

But he did need money.

Dillon wasn't about to ask Natalie to pay up for babysitting her sister. He didn't feel right about taking money for his time with Hope anyway. However, he did want to finish his painting job as quickly as possible so he could get his cash and go.

At the moment, he only had enough money to travel maybe two states away by bus. Once he was paid, he could add at least a couple more states as cushion. Or maybe Mexico would be good.

Just getting out of Garden Cottage for an hour or two would help him breathe a little better though. Especially today—the day of Grandad's funeral.

Slapping on a pair of sunglasses and a baseball hat, Dillon charged out of the house and tore the car down the gravel drive-way. Knuckles white on the steering wheel and chest numb, he drove.

He wanted to stay away from any place where he might run into funeral-goers. He wanted to stay away from anyone who might recognize him. Really, he did.

Then how did he end up a block down from the Sanders Hotel?

Dillon shifted the car into park but kept the engine running. He could see people coming and going through the entrance of the hotel.

He recalled one summer vacation right after he'd turned nine, jumping out of his parents' car, running up the few short steps, through the revolving glass door and stopping in the middle of the hotel foyer yelling, "I'm back!"

The staff had laughed, and Grandad had walked down the grand staircase and messed up his hair, saying with a grin, "Yes, you are! Welcome home, my boy."

There had been no doubt in Dillon's mind where he belonged. Where was home.

Shaking away the sudden memory he usually stuffed away so deep he couldn't see or touch it, he shifted the car out of park and was about to press the gas pedal when he realized someone was standing in front of his car. He slammed on the brakes out of reflex even though he hadn't even rolled forward and shoved the gear back into park.

Blood pulsing, Dillon rolled down the window. "Ms. Fi! What are you doing? I could have run into you!"

Nonplussed, Fiona met him at his window. Her eyes were ringed with thick, smudged mascara, and her hair looked even more orange-red against her black hat and dress that was accentuated with multi-colored buttons. "I'm sorry I startled you, dear. I was helping with the food and forgot a pound cake I left in the trunk." She reached into the car and grasped his hand. "Oh, Dillon, I'm so glad you came."

"I didn't come. I mean, I'm not coming." He bit back a moan. "I just needed to take a ride. I'm actually leaving in a day or two." He added the last bit so she wouldn't get her hopes up about him staying permanently.

Her eyes widened, but she didn't pull back. "But what about Hope?"

He tensed, slowly sliding his hand away. "What about her?"

"You've been reading to her."

Dillon pulled the brim of his cap further down. "Yes, but Natalie's back now. She can read to her if she wants."

Fiona's small chin wobbled slightly. "The poor girl. She's been through a lot and needs a friend. I try to spend as much time as I can visiting with her, but I have other patients too." She sighed, the black feather in her hat quivering. "And her sister, dear thing, spends as much time as she can, but she never knows when she has to work and," she lowered her voice though no one else was around, "I believe she feels some guilt over what happened, so she finds it hard to spend time with her sister."

Though itching to leave, this caught Dillon's attention. He asked the question he'd been dying to know, "What happened?"

At this, Fiona's thin, arched brows furrowed. "Well, I wasn't there, but from what I was told, it happened at your brother and Natalie's reception at the Sanders Hotel, and you know, the wide, sweeping staircase in the grand foyer?"

When Dillon nodded, she continued, "Hope somehow tumbled down those stairs and fell in a heap at the bottom. She hit her head and has been in a coma ever since."

"'Somehow'?" He hadn't missed the doubt in Fiona's voice and the moisture edging her eyes.

She bit her lip and blinked, her expression as serious as Dillon had ever seen on her. "Something just doesn't sit quite right is all. Parker and Natalie have been mum about the whole thing and glossed over things with the press. Which doesn't make them too happy, you know."

Yes, he did know. Before she could explain more, he caught sight of a group headed their way in funeral clothing. Anxiousness crept up his spine. "I'm sorry, Ms. Fi, but I have to go." He shifted the car in drive again.

Fiona gazed at him with unnerving calm. "Alright, sweetie, but feel free to drop by the nursing home to visit anytime." She grasped the edge of the window before he could raise it all the way. "Awake or asleep, I'm sure Hope enjoys when a friend visits."

Dillon paused, muscles shifting in his throat as he tried to swallow. "As I said, I'll be leaving soon. But thanks, Ms. Fi, for everything."

Natalie

"Dillon was here?"

Natalie clamped her lips shut, carefully glancing around to see if anyone had heard her exclamation. Thankfully, her and Fiona stood in a fairly secluded corner of the hotel kitchen. The rest of the staff were distracted. She had escaped for a few moments for a breather to find Fiona getting in the thick of everything and taking it upon herself to gather more glasses of sweet tea.

She lowered her voice to a whisper. "Dillon was really here?"

Fiona continued filling cups with ice. "Yes, dear. He was parked outside when I arrived."

Hope and worry pulsed through Natalie's being. Hope, because maybe Dillon's visit meant he was softening to the idea of reuniting with his family. And worry, because if Parker's reaction was any indication of how people would receive Dillon back, it wouldn't be pretty.

"He said he'd be leaving in a couple days."

Natalie snapped to attention to see Fiona watching her with a worry line puckering between her brows. Her hopes plummeted. "He did?" Chewing on her bottom lip, she grabbed a glass filled with iced tea and took a long swig before setting it back down. "I don't know what to do, Fiona."

The older woman gave her a sympathizing look. "All I know to do is love the boy and pray my heart out."

Natalie twisted the glass on the stainless steel countertop, leaving circles of condensation. "The only prayer I've known how to pray lately is 'God, what should I do?'"

"That's not a bad prayer. Not a bad one at all. He likes it when we ask Him questions. Means we want Him to answer, and He always gives us one."

She sighed, longing to change out of her tight, black dress and high heels and go for a run. "I just wish I knew if I wanted the answer or not."

Fiona raised an eyebrow and picked up a tray filled with a pitcher of tea and cups of ice. "One way to find out." Balancing the tray with one hand, she patted Natalie cheek. "Peace, sweetie." She swished out of the room.

Natalie sipped her tea a minute, ignoring her phone as it buzzed in her clutch purse. It was probably Beth again. She'd been trying to get her to talk about Dillon and the Sanders family drama for days. She toyed with the idea of answering. It would be nice to talk with her best friend right now.

Choosing to ignore the phone call, she let out a breath. "Okay." Casting her eyes heavenward, she released a prayer born out of her struggling new faith. *God, what should I do?*

Only the sounds of pots and pans clanging at the other end of the kitchen filled her ears.

Slinging back the last of her tea, she set the glass back on the counter with a thump. All she really wanted to do was stop keeping all of her brother-in-law's secrets and be honest with her husband about Dillon leaving.

She raised her eyebrows. Was that an answer?

As if in confirmation, Parker walked through the swinging kitchen door. He stopped in the midst of loosening his tie when he saw her. "Hi," he said stiffly.

Her heart sank at his detached tone. "Hi." She tapped her fingers on her leg. "Needed some space?"

"If you don't mind."

She'd actually meant space from the few hundred or so guests in the other room, but okay…No. She took a deep breath and blurted out, "Dillon's planning to leave tomorrow or the next day."

Parker's face paled.

"Fiona just told me," she said. "He was just here."

"Here?"

"Outside. He left though."

Letting out a low growl, he turned on his heel and charged out the door.

After blinking in place for a split second, she ran after him. "Where are you going?"

Parker loosened his tie further, ignoring the bewildered stares of those they breezed past. He answered in a low but tight voice, "To beat up my little brother."

When they blew through the front entrance, Natalie grabbed his arm. "Wait. I'll drive."

He frowned. "You don't need to come."

She refrained from rolling her eyes. "Yes, I do. You don't know the way to Garden Cottage, remember?" Leading the way to Parker's rental car, she tossed over her shoulder, "And I need to act as referee. We don't need you two killing each other. Especially today."

The ride to Garden Cottage was tense. Natalie didn't even try to diffuse her boiling pot of a husband. She knew opening her mouth would set him off more. Truth was, she was a little scared of him. She'd seen him angry but never this livid.

Her phone rang, causing both of them to jump. She immediately turned the ringer down, noticing it was Beth again.

When they reached Garden Cottage, she was almost disappointed to see the Sedan she'd loaned Dillon sitting in the driveway. A part of her had hoped he would still be driving around, giving Parker time to cool off. No such luck.

The car was barely in park before Parker blasted up the front steps and banged on the door. Natalie scrambled to pull her keys out of the ignition and joined him.

The front door opened, revealing Dillon with a neutral expression on his face. He must have seen them drive up. "I thought you'd still be at the reception."

Parker hit him.

Natalie's hands flew to her mouth as the younger Sanders brother stumbled back under the force of the blow.

"You should have been at the reception!" Parker yelled, his

face beet red and landing another punch, this time in his brother's stomach. "And at the funeral. And at home the last two years!"

"Parker, stop!" Natalie cried out when she saw Dillon wasn't fighting back. Blood dripped from his nose. He almost looked resigned to his beating.

Fists buried in his brother's shirt, Parker glanced at her, his eyes wet and red-rimmed. Her own eyes filled with tears.

Letting out a frustrated groan, he slammed Dillon into the wall. "Just tell me why." His voice was heavy with exhaustion. "Why did you leave and why do you keep running away?"

Dillon stared at him, his face a hard mask but his eyes flicking over his normally even-keeled brother's face.

"Why?" Parker asked, practically shaking him.

"It was me!" Dillon finally screamed, causing Natalie to jump. "I was the hit-and-run driver."

The air was sucked out of the room.

"What?" Parker choked out.

"I was the one who hit Mom. I was the one who put her in that wheelchair. I took away her ability to walk, to talk, to laugh." He let out a shaky laugh, devoid of humor "She was driving fast, I wasn't paying attention, I hit her. Then I ran away because I was scared and kept quiet. But the guilt ate me up inside, and I knew it would kill our family for anyone to find out, so I left." He jerked out of Parker's loosened grip and smoothed his shirt. "Are you happy now?"

All the fight seemed to have left Parker, leaving his shoulders sagging as he stared at his brother in disbelief. "It was you?"

Dillon's face hardened as if that were the worst possible thing he could have said. Without another word, he grabbed a set of keys from the side table and swept out the front door. They could hear the engine roar to life and him peal down the driveway before heavy silence descended.

Natalie took a tentative step forward. "Park—"

He held up his hand, closing his eyes. Her throat tightened.

"Just," he walked over to the open front door and stared with a vacant gaze, "give me a minute." The door shut softly behind him as he walked outside.

Through the window, Natalie could see him sink down on the front porch steps and run his hands over his face. She flinched when her phone began buzzing in her hand. She hadn't even realized she'd brought it in with her.

It was Beth.

This time she answered. "Hey."

"Nat, finally! Why have you been ignoring my calls? Listen, I—wait, are you crying?"

As soon as she'd heard her friend's voice hot tears had cascaded down her face and choked her throat. "Yes."

"Oh, honey, was the funeral rough?"

Natalie sniffed, turning away from the window. "This isn't about the funeral."

"Then, what's wrong?"

She told her everything.

A great Hope fell
You heard no noise
The Ruin was within
Oh cunning wreck that told no tale
And let no Witness in
—Emily Dickinson

CHAPTER EIGHTEEN

Hope

I sucked in a breath, choking on wet air. "Where did he go?"

Gardener placed a hand on my shoulder, peering with me into the fog. "He's gone."

The way he said it made my heart jump into my throat. "He ran away, but…" I didn't want to voice my question. Would he come back?

I asked a different one instead. "How do we get out of here?"

Gardener tapped his ear. "Follow the sound of water."

Water?

Closing my eyes, I tipped my head to the side, listening. Sure enough, I heard the sound of rushing water somewhere nearby. I opened my eyes. "Is it a river?"

"And more." He walked with purposeful steps through the blinding fog.

Though he was confident following the sound of an invisible river, I was still disoriented. Grabbing the edge of his sleeve, I followed close beside him.

After several minutes of walking, the roar of Gardener's something "more" became apparent, and we emerged from the fog next to a river that fell over a cliff in a twenty-foot waterfall.

"Wow," I whispered. A double-rainbow arced over the cliff in the waterfall's spray.

In that one moment, the fear that had latched onto me in the fog began to unwind, allowing me to breathe freely again. Just for one moment, before it wrapped back around me tighter than ever.

With a swift turn, I put my back to the rainbow and faced the fog again. "What was that?" My voice pitched higher than normal.

Gardener placed a protective arm in front of me as his brow furrowed.

A slight parting in the mist revealed the glinting eyes of what looked like a crouching lion.

The hair on my neck rose when I heard its menacing snarl.

"Don't move," Gardener warned, his voice ringing with author-itative steel.

In my panicked haze, I wasn't sure whether he was command-ing me or the lion, but my body reacted before my mind. I turned and ran.

The lion let out a low roar, and I felt the slight tremble in the ground when it bounded after me.

I chanced a look over my shoulder. Everything moved as if in slow motion. It was the dark path all over again, but this time the darkness had taken the form of a lion.

This time I had Gardener.

He ran between me and the lion, waving his arms.

"No!" I cried out. He'd be ripped to shreds.

The lion's stride slowed but not much, and the cliff was drawing near. I had to make a choice.

Heart racing in my chest, I knew I had to jump. Last time, I hid behind a door for safety. This time I had to gather more bravery and jump over a waterfall.

I could do this.

Yelling over my shoulder at Gardener, I prepared to leap over the cliff. "We have to jump! Run!"

He looked back, and I took that as a signal he heard me. There was no time to lose. The lion's hungry eyes were drawing closer.

"Wait!" Gardener called out.

Wait? Frowning, I almost turned back. Instead, I drew in a sharp breath and dove off the cliff. For a solid moment I was airborne, completely still between earth and sky.

I fell.

Beads of hard water bit my eyes. Cold air froze my lungs. The impact of hitting the lake below jarred my body.

I surfaced coughing. Looking above, I couldn't see anything through the hazy waterfall mist. I couldn't tell if Gardener had jumped or not.

After another coughing fit, it took me a couple minutes to swim to shore. I collapsed in a shivering—but safe—mass.

Just as I gathered enough strength to crawl to my knees, a voice called out. The Gardener's voice.

"Here I am!" I responded, my own voice coming out like a croak. Scrambling to my feet, I cleared my throat and tried again. "I'm over here!"

Though I could see an open field on the far side of the lake, the part where I'd climbed ashore was surrounded by dense woods like at the top of the cliff. Giddy relief surged through me when I saw Gardener emerge from the woody depths with Dickinson's basket on his arm.

I lifted my arms in the air with a wide smile stretching my face. "We made it!" Laughing, I did a little twirl, scattering water droplets everywhere. "And I jumped over a waterfall! Did you see?" I stopped twirling with a breathless huff. "How did you get away?"

"What were you thinking?" Gardener's quiet voice and serious expression made my smile slip.

"I needed to get away from the lion." I frowned, searching his eyes. "Didn't you want me to be safe?"

"You *were* safe."

What? I jerked my arm toward the cliff. "There was a crazed lion chasing us, and the only escape was to jump. It was the bravest thing I've ever done!"

"No!" Gardener's voice came out sharp and firm. "That wasn't bravery. It was fear."

A water droplet ran down the bridge of my nose. I wrapped my arms around myself, hunching my shoulders. "Why are you so angry? We're alright."

"If you keep wanting to run away you won't always be." His intense gaze softened. "There's a time to run and a time to stand still. Did you even wonder why I told you to not move and to wait?"

I blinked. "A little, but I thought…" My voice trailed off. I didn't know what I was thinking.

"I'll tell you what I was thinking. I was thinking Dickinson never would have survived a jump over the waterfall, and if I'd left him alone, he never would have survived the lion. I couldn't abandon him."

Locking my gaze on the bluebird, I remembered one crucial detail. "And you're the Gardener. The animals will listen to you." I lifted my gaze. "The lion listened and went away without a fight, didn't it?"

He nodded. "Yes."

Sinking to the ground on shaking knees, I finally realized that I'd abandoned the only two friends who hadn't left me. "I'm sorry," I whispered, moisture choking my voice.

Gardener kneeled in front of me, swiping a runaway tear from my cheek. "I didn't tell you this to shame you, but show you what you're capable of. You're already brave. There's no need to prove that to yourself or anyone else. If you had trusted me and realized there are things more important than being afraid, fear wouldn't have had control over you."

"You think I'm brave?" I had done nothing I could remember to prove it.

He gave me his warm smile, effectively melting away any shame I felt. "Of course."

With those two words, I felt a burden release from my spirit, and I could believe it too. I was ready for the next leg of our journey. "So, where can we find Dillon?"

Gardener raised an eyebrow. Without commenting, he reached into his pocket and pulled out an object, allowing it to dangle from a piece of corded leather in front of my eyes.

A brass key. Its top shaped like a three-leafed clover.

I swallowed hard, wrapping my fingers around it, and he released the cord. "He's headed for the gate?"

Standing, Gardener offered me his hand. After pulling the cord over my head so the key hung from around my neck, I allowed him to help me to my feet.

Away we go.

Dillon

It was a fairly secluded road. A back way to avoid some of the Atlanta traffic.

Dillon parked the rented Sedan on the side of the road and got out, finally giving the engine a rest after driving straight through to Atlanta. He'd only stopped once for gas and to wash his face since he startled the cashier half to death with his bloodied nose and black eye.

Leaning back against the car, he focused on the road that curved in front of him, lit up only by dim streetlights every quarter mile and his car's headlights.

Car headlights.

When he recalled each of his recent dreams, the only part that made sense to him was the car. He saw those headlights coming toward him all the time, awake or asleep. The image seemed to be seared into his brain.

The accident happened the first week of his senior year. It was a rainy Friday night, and he was returning home from a party. He was sober and never texted while he drove, but he looked down for a couple seconds to mess with the radio when she came tearing around the bend.

Everything happened fast except for those first few moments when he looked up and saw the headlights flash across his windshield. The pavement was wet, she had taken the curve too quickly, he had drifted toward the middle of the road, and they collided.

He spun. She flipped.

Shaken, but not injured except for knocking his head on the steering wheel, Dillon had climbed out of his Mustang, the scent of something wet and burning stinging his nostrils. He took five steps before he realized it was his mother's car. Another seven steps took him to the upside-down driver's side window to see her crumpled body.

Spotting her scratched-up phone on the pavement amongst crushed glass, he dialed for an ambulance with shaking fingers as he grasped her wrist to take her pulse. Dillon could have sworn she didn't have one.

He panicked.

Hearing the voice of the dispatcher on the other end of the line, he'd dropped the phone without responding and ran.

Investigating the nature of the call, the police found her, barely alive. In the months following, Dillon could barely even stand to look at his mother under the burden of his secret. If he had only left his radio alone, if he had only stayed with her even when he thought she was gone. If only he had owned up to being there.

It was an accident. He knew that was true. The choices he made after, however, could have been different.

And the choices now?

Dillon sank to his knees in the middle of the lonely road, pressing the palm of his hand against the spot where the collision had taken place. His eyes and throat burned, but he refused to crumble.

I'm sorry, he mouthed, sound refusing to emit from his tight throat.

Of whom he was asking forgiveness, he wasn't certain. Mom? God? Himself? He knew none would give it.

The quality of mercy is not strain'd...

He could almost hear Grandad whisper the words in his ear.

"Mercy?" Dillon choked on the word. He yelled out, pounding a closed fist to his chest, "I don't deserve mercy!"

It is enthroned in the hearts of kings...

Grandad said Dad still took care of those birdhouses they built together. Why did he do that?

It is an attribute to God himself...

Wishes and prayers.

"I'm a coward and selfish." Bowing his head, his voice broke. "I deserve this. I deserve to be alone." He pushed to his feet. "I deserve to suffer."

The low hum of an approaching vehicle charged the air and shook the ground.

For a long, frozen moment, Dillon stayed rooted in the middle of the road, waiting for the vehicle to swing around the curve in the road. They wouldn't even have time to swerve.

Though justice be thy plea, consider this that, in the course of justice, none of us should see salvation...

Snapping out of his trance, he broke into a stumbling run to the Sedan. Breathing heavily, he threw himself inside just as the car appeared and zoomed by. The driver was completely unaware Dillon had been standing there.

Dillon groaned, dragging trembling hands down his face. What was he doing?

Was he trying to recreate his dreams? Striving for the ending he always knew he deserved? If this really had been his dream, Hope would have appeared, standing in his way.

Hope.

Blindly reaching into the passenger's side of the car, he pulled a book off the seat and snapped on the interior light. He never did finish reading *Peter Pan* to her.

Turning to the end, he ran his fingers over the handwritten words then paused. Hope hadn't written comments about the story but a prayer.

> *God, I forgive him. I do. I forgive them all. I forgive Mom for abandoning us. I forgive Natalie for leaving (I know she had to). And finally, I forgive Dad for being so blinded by his own grief and fear that he hurts all those around him. Especially me, locking me away like Rapunzel in her tower, convinced I'll run too.*

Dillon's grip tightened on the book edges. What did she mean? Locked away?

> *But can I forgive myself for not running? For not being stronger, braver? I have to forgive if I want to keep moving forward. If I want to keep breathing. 'While I breathe, I hope.' My teacher, Mrs. Sanders, shared that quote with me. I should make it my life quote.*

Sucking in a sharp breath, he reread the last few lines. Black spots danced around the corners of his vision as he stared hard at the words, afraid they'd disappear like a figment from a dream.

Mrs. Sanders. Mom was her teacher? She did used to teach summers in Mobile. And the quote...the Dillon motto.

Running a shaky hand through his hair, he read the last of the prayer in a daze.

> *I pray mercy and grace for my family. I pray for hope so I can keep breathing. Jesus, give me patience for the right time and courage to do what I need to do. I can't stay stuck here forever. Never is an awfully long time...*

Dillon read Hope's prayer at least a dozen times. He couldn't shy away from this any longer. He'd shoved aside the very obvious fact that this girl needed help.

And so did he.

For some reason, they were meant to help each other.

Dillon texted Natalie and told her to meet him at the airport in Mobile. A sense of urgency tugged at him and not a small amount of fear.

Going back to Mobile and contacting Natalie most likely meant seeing his family again. But he had prayed for direction, and he got it. Dillon had been ignoring God, but maybe He wasn't ignoring him.

If that were the case...

We do pray for mercy...

Why must people kneel down to pray? If I really wanted to pray I'll
tell you what I'd do. I'd go out into a great big field all alone or in
the deep,
deep woods and I'd look up into the sky—up—up—up—into that
lovely
blue sky that looks as if there was no end to its blueness.
And then I'd just feel a prayer.
L.M. Montgomery, *Anne of Green Gables*

CHAPTER NINETEEN

Parker

After a sleepless night, Parker found himself standing in the middle of his parents' suite staring at his father in disbelief.

"Are you saying you knew Dillon was the hit-and-run driver?"

Casting a long glance at the closed door of the bedroom where Carol was still sleeping, Jacob sank down on the suede couch. "Yes." His voice was weary.

Parker had to sit down too. Wasn't there a limit on how many revelations a person could take before going completely over the edge?

"The night before Dillon left," his father said, "I found him attempting to steal money out of the safe in my home study."

Could his brother dig his grave any deeper?

Jacob continued, "He told me he was leaving and taking the money intended for his education. We argued. He confessed." He propped his elbows on his knees, a wry smile tilting his lips. "It probably was a lot like the fight you had with him yesterday."

Not unless he gave Dillon a bloody nose. "He told you he hit Mom?"

"I guessed it." Jacob sighed. "I know you boys. So does your mother. After the accident, we all took it hard, but Dillon reacted a bit differently. It was little things. He avoided eye contact. Didn't laugh anymore, rarely smiled. Visited your mother in the hospital and rehab less and less. He took to his workshop, hardly ever coming out."

"Guilt," Parker murmured, a bit surprised he hadn't recognized it himself. He was blinded by his own worry and newfound responsibilities.

His father nodded. "Yes, but it wasn't until that night, looking straight into his eyes—I knew."

"How did you react?"

"I said, 'It was you.'"

Parker shut his eyes. "I said the same thing." No wonder Dillon had looked haunted. He was reliving the moment with their dad. All the guilt, fresh again. "It wasn't the best thing I could have said, was it?"

Jacob leaned back, sinking into the couch cushion. "It's a natural shocked reaction, I think. The problem was, I didn't say anything after." Tiredness etched lines into his face.

"We just stood there…staring at each other. Me, waiting for his apology. Him, waiting for my forgiveness. We both said nothing."

"Isn't that normal though? Wanting him to apologize first?"

"Normal is over-rated. Pride and fairness be hanged. If I had spoken up first, I may have had my son these last couple years. He left before I could."

"Does Mom know?"

"No, I was worried it might interfere with the progress she was making. It was enough that he left, I don't know how she would have handled the reason."

Parker couldn't let go of one thing though. "Why didn't you tell me?" He raked a hand through his hair, sure the strands were sticking straight up by now. "I don't understand all the secrecy." He was getting pretty sick of it actually.

"For a while, I thought your brother was coming back. He was always a homebody. I couldn't imagine him staying away as long as he did. When it became obvious he wasn't, well, so much time had passed already. Everyone had moved on. Come to their own conclusions."

"You still could have told me. No matter how much time had passed." Parker leaned forward. "You *should* have told me."

Jacob locked gazes with him. "Son, I know I made mistakes, and I am sorry. I could have handled everything differently. Hindsight is 20/20. But now…now we move forward. Do the best we can. Are you willing to do that?"

Parker drew in a deep breath through his nose and let it out slowly. "Is our family ready to be completely honest? Because I don't think I can handle any more secrets and lies."

"Yes, and we—" His father released a heavy sigh, shoulders sagging. "We will tell your mother, but I still believe Dillon should be the one to come clean about his past actions. We keep this in-house for the time being."

"And if he never does?"

Jacob gave him a steady look. "It's still our family's business, don't you think? No need broadcasting everything to everyone unless necessary."

"In theory, I do agree, but—" Parker hesitated. "If there's anything I found out this week, it's that eventually everything comes into the light."

Hope

I couldn't remember the last time I felt like this. Excitement pumped through my veins at such a heady speed I almost felt lightheaded.

We had crested a hill that swooped below to an open field of golden green grass stretching far into the horizon. Wildflowers added splashes of color, swaying in the strong wind that buffeted my dress and tugged playfully at my hair.

Gardener came up beside me. "You like it?" The proud smile in his voice made me think he created the space just for me.

"It's so…" I struggled to find the right word. "Open." I flashed him a grin. "I love it."

The ruggedness of his features was more apparent in this wide, open space. It was like he was part of his surroundings. Or they were part of him.

Closing my eyes, I breathed in deeply. Spicy, sharp, and fresh.

Where the garden was comfort and beauty, this meadow was wildness and freedom.

The perfect place to dance.

As though reading my thoughts, Gardener let out a loud whoop, startling my eyes open. Throwing me an impish grin, he sprinted down the hill, arms spread wide at his side like wings. When he reached the bottom, he cut a flip before landing solidly on his feet. He waved for me to join him.

I looked at Dickinson, who was fluffing his feathers as though itching to leave his basket. "Soon, buddy," I promised, before taking off into the field.

I was able to slow my speed near the base of the hill enough to gently deposit Dickinson's basket on the ground before I flew into Gardener's arms.

Letting out a deep, belly laugh, he whirled me around in a breathless circle before setting me back on my feet again. I immediately took off.

Running and *running away* are two very different things. I had become accustomed to sprinting away in fear or panic, but running without limit and feeling the air rush past you for the joy of it? Glorious. Better than jumping off the highest cliff.

Gardener kept pace with me while I ran as fast as I could. When I couldn't run anymore, I spun with my arms raised, embracing the sky. My dress whipped around my legs as I twirled. Then, finally, I was dancing.

True dancing isn't thinking, but breathing. Pure and instinctual movement. Trusting your body to respond to the feelings and expression in your heart and mind. It can be messy. It can be beautiful.

It's life in motion.

I hadn't truly let myself experience life in a long time.

After what seemed like hours, I collapsed back into the grass, skin flushed. Gardener had disappeared somewhere, but I wasn't alarmed. He'd probably just gone to fetch Dickinson.

I was proved half-right when a few minutes later a shadow hovered over me, tickling my face with a bouquet of wildflowers. Giggling, I snatched them into my lap and sat up.

Gardener hooked a leg beneath him and settled down a couple feet away, setting Dickinson's basket between us. "Having fun?"

"Mmm." I just gave him a big smile, pressing a marigold to my lips.

He extracted the bluebird from the basket. "I think we can take his binding off now."

I dropped the flower back into my lap and scooted closer. "Really? Will he be able to fly now? Is he ready for that?" Excitement and nervousness warred for dominance as I absently picked at my own bandages.

After the last of the cloth had been loosened, Dickinson fidgeted while Gardener examined his wing. "Almost," was his diagnosis. "It's still a little weak, but we'll keep the wing free as it strengthens."

My shoulders sagged. I wasn't sure if it was in disappointment or relief. I wanted Dickinson well, but I'd also miss him if he flew away and I never saw him again.

Fingering the bouquet in my lap, I said, "I think I'll make another flower crown since my last one got ruined when I…jumped earlier." I spared him a sheepish glance.

He didn't even flinch, opting to stretch out in the grass. "Good idea."

Weaving and tying together a collection of meadowsweet, red poppies, marigolds, and wild daisies, the new crown turned out more colorful and fanciful-looking than my previous one. I settled it in my hair with an air of satisfaction.

Gardener propped himself up on his elbows and gave me an appraising look. "Lovely."

I twisted a lock of my hair between my fingers. "Really?"

His eyes softened, turning a deep blue-green with shimmers of gold like the surrounding meadow and sky. "Of course." Standing, he picked up the basket and offered to help me up. "Are you ready?"

I eyed his outstretched hand with a dubious look but took it anyway. "Ready for what?"

Pulling me to my feet, he gave me a side-squeeze. "For the rest of our journey." He pointed at a shadowed outline in the distance. I couldn't tell if they were rocks or trees.

My hand instinctively reached for the key hanging about my neck. "Are we close?"

"Not far now."

We delight in the beauty of a butterfly, but rarely admit the changes it has gone through to achieve that beauty.
—Maya Angelou

CHAPTER TWENTY

Dillon

"So what is this all about?" Natalie asked as they entered Garden Cottage. Early morning sunlight streamed through windows, painting everything yellow. "You disappear then fly back, only to barely say two words to me on the ride from the airport."

"Sorry, but I wanted to check something before I asked you a question." Dillon strode through the living area and kitchen until he knelt in front of Hope's bedroom door. He ran his fingers across the doorknob, a frown puckering his brow. "Does the door to the master bedroom lock from the outside?"

Natalie cast him a curious glance before checking. "No, why?"

"Then why does Hope's?" He pulled out the copy of *Peter Pan* from his jacket, flipped to the last page and thrust it at her. "Here, read this."

When she received the book with a tentative hand, he entered the bedroom and began pulling other books off the shelves, piling them on the bed.

"What do you think you're doing?" Natalie asked, standing in the doorway with wide eyes.

"Looking for more answers." Dillon waved a hand toward the book she was holding. "Just read what Hope wrote, and you'll understand."

"What she wrote?" Natalie murmured but did as he said.

As she read, he flipped through pages, trying to find more than just commentary. After several minutes of searching, he looked up to see her sink into the desk chair, gripping the back with white fingers.

Setting the book he was reading in his lap, he tried to word his next question as carefully as possible, "You've suspected all along your dad was involved in Hope's accident, didn't you?"

Natalie flinched and closed her eyes. She nodded. "But I prayed I was wrong."

Dillon pulled the picture of the young sisters out of his pocket and handed it to her. "What happened?"

Her eyes glistened as she gazed at the photograph. "You know, this was the last day my family was really happy. At least, I thought we were." With a soft sigh, she set the picture on the desk and faced him. "My mom left the next day. She left a letter explaining she'd—" Natalie held up her fingers like air quotes, "—'lost herself,' and needed to explore her options, or whatever."

"She seriously said she needed to find herself?"

Natalie gave him a pointed look. "We all get a little lost at some point in our lives."

A flush pricked the back of his neck. No argument there. He said softly, "That doesn't excuse bad choices."

Gazing at him for a long moment, she finally replied, "No, no it doesn't." She picked at a piece of lint on her black pants. "Did you ever wonder why I was willing to help you and keep your secret to the extent that I did?"

"For Parker's sake?" Dillon set the book he was holding aside, picking up another—*The Little White Horse* by Elizabeth Goudge.

She pressed her lips together. "If I had done anything for Parker, it would have been telling him the truth right away. But, no." Walking over to the bed, she settled on the floor and grabbed a novel from the pile. "I was falling back into old habits."

He remembered Hope's prayer. "You ran away too?"

"After Mom left, my dad changed. He'd always been the one to take charge, but he became more controlling. He lowered our curfews and was really strict with how we spent our time away from home, which was fine except then he started grounding us for little things. Worthless things. Just making excuses for us to not go out. I think in the back of his mind, he was afraid we'd leave him too."

"But he held on too tight."

"Yeah," she said softly, opening the book and staring blankly at the page. "It didn't seem to bother Hope as much. She'd always been a homebody, but I felt like I was slowly being suffocated. The day I turned eighteen felt like a get-out-of-jail-free card."

"You left."

"To go to college," Natalie said, her voice defensive. She tilted her head up to give him a hard stare. "My dad was never cruel, just controlling. Even though he didn't like it, he didn't keep me from leaving, though he probably wanted to. I didn't leave on the best terms, but I did not abandon my sister."

Dillon stared right back. "Not to sound like a hypocrite, but did you ever come back, even for visits?"

She paled a bit before facing forward again. "I sent emails."

Silence stretched taut between them before Dillon broke it. "Hey, I'm the last person to judge."

Natalie's lips twitched as though trying to smirk but failed. "Yes, you are." She held up the book. "Now, tell me what we're looking for?"

"You don't have any definitive proof about your dad being involved with Hope's accident, right?"

"No, he could have been at the wedding, but none of the cameras caught him at the hotel, from what we could see anyway. When we tried to find him at home…" She shrugged. "He was gone. Haven't seen him since."

"Strange."

"The only real clue that Hope didn't simply trip down the stairs was the mirror in the bridal suite." She chewed the corner of her lip. "It was shattered beyond repair, and there were spots of Hope's blood on the floor and on some of the pieces. We kept that information from the press."

Dillon's stomach clenched, the muscle in his jaw twitching. He opened the novel in his lap. "I was thinking Hope may have written a clue in her books somewhere. Something that could help clarify things." And maybe she'd mention his mom again. He hesitated. "Natalie?"

She looked up. "Yeah?"

"Did you know Mom was Hope's teacher?"

Her brow furrowed. "No, I had no idea."

"Strange," he muttered again before they dove back into Hope's writings.

For nearly an hour, the only sound was the rustle of turning pages.

Dillon finally found one entry that he knelt on the floor to show Natalie.

Dad threw away my journals today, so I've had to resort to writing in my books. He said writing "put ideas" into my head, which I don't understand because I'm taking MY ideas OUT of my head and putting them onto paper. But I don't think he quite understood what he was saying either—since he was so drunk.

Natalie gasped, pressing a hand to her mouth. "When did he start drinking?"

It doesn't help that mom was a writer too. It probably brought back bad memories for him. Is this considered dishonoring my father by writing in secret? No, I don't believe so. He was wrong to throw away my journals. My thoughts. My dreams. My prayers.

Oh, I know those are inside of me, but I couldn't help but feel pain and emptiness as he took almost four years of my life and threw them in the garbage. I cried and tried to stop him, but he just slapped me and shoved me into my room, locking the door behind him as he left. He added the lock the day after Natalie left without saying goodbye to him. He thinks I'll run away too.

Tears were streaming down Natalie's face, but Dillon kept reading to the end.

I'm only allowed to go to and from school now. I even had to miss school some days when he was too hung-over to take me. I may have to go during the summer if this keeps up.

Now my only friends are God and the characters in my books. Good ones, if I say so myself. Doesn't mean I don't still get lonely though…

Surging to her feet, Natalie paced the room. "Why didn't she tell me this in our emails?"

Dillon was still distracted by Hope's mention of summer school. Was that when she met Mom? "Um…he probably read over her emails before she sent them." He picked up another book, *Ballet Shoes*. Little Hope from his dream twirled across his memory. "Hope liked to dance, didn't she?"

Natalie stopped pacing and frowned at him, her brow crimping. "Yes, she loved to dance. How did you-what's wrong?"

He knew his face must have looked sheet white. She knelt beside him, but he didn't look up from Hope's words.

It's my fault. I wondered why she didn't come.

I was able to hide one of the portable phones in my bedroom last night before Dad locked the door. When I was sure he was sleeping, I hid in my closet and called Mrs. Sanders. She was so kind to me over the summer. I think she suspected something was wrong, but I never found a good opportunity to tell her.

I spilled everything as soon as she answered. Dad's drunken fits have been coming more and more often lately. He hasn't done more than yelling, grabbing my arm hard or slapping my face twice, but lately he's been getting worse. It scares me.

Mrs. Sanders surprised me by asking if I could leave tonight. She could catch a plane to Mobile and pick me up in just a couple hours. The idea was so thrilling and terrifying, but I agreed, planning where to meet her. After sneaking out the window, I waited almost all night at the Waffle House down the road before Dad found me. I wish I had told someone, anyone else, I needed help, even the police, but I was foolish and trust isn't my strongest suit. Only Mrs. Sanders had gained it.

When we got home...he never hit me so hard before. He's putting bars on all the windows now. I'll never be free.

But why am I pitying myself? Mrs. Sanders' accident was on the news this morning. I know she was on her way to help me.

It's my fault. If I had just been brave enough to ask for help sooner...

Maybe I deserve this.

Dillon couldn't feel Natalie's hand gripping his shoulder. He could hardly breathe. The words blurred. He shut his eyes and the vision of his mom's speeding car tore through his mind.

"She was going to tell me about Dad," Natalie's choked voice pierced the shocked fog clouding his mind. "At my wedding."

"Wait." Shifting, he faced her, his gaze penetrating. "If Hope was locked up, and your dad wasn't there, how did she make it to your wedding without him?"

They stared at each other for several heartbeats before Dillon jumped to his feet and strode to the window. "Look, there! One of the window bars is missing. There's enough room for Hope to squeeze out."

Natalie came up beside him. "You think she was able to run away again?"

His mouth set in a grim line, reluctant to speak aloud his next words, "That would be one way to make your dad really angry."

She bit her lip and seemed about to say something when she got distracted. "Someone's in the backyard."

Dillon peered out the window and saw Jan-di hoofing it through the overgrown grass, one hand pressed to her belly. She looked out of breath and anxious. He met her at the back door. "Hey, is everything okay?"

Her gaze went passed him to Natalie.

"Oh, Jan-di, this is—"

"Nat," the petite Asian woman interrupted him, "where's your television?"

Natalie inclined her head toward the living room. "This way."

Jan-di followed her inside, leaving Dillon floored. "Wait, you two know each other?"

"Cooper is Hope's doctor," Natalie explained, distracted. "Where's the remote?"

"On the recliner." He turned to Jan-di. "So you knew who I was the whole time?"

She shrugged, sinking onto the edge of the couch with a relieved sigh. "She just told me Garden Cottage had a new tenant for a while and to keep an eye on you." She winked. "So I put you to work. You've been doing a great job by the way."

"Neighborhood watch," Dillon muttered as Natalie switched to the channel Jan-di directed her to.

They all fell silent as an old picture of Dillon flashed across the screen with the words: The Prodigal Son Returns.

"Oh. My. Gosh." Natalie fell back onto the recliner.

Dillon's hands tingled and a buzzing began in his ears. The reporter's voice seemed to come from far away.

"It's been reported that Dillon Sanders, age nineteen, has finally returned home after disappearing over two years ago after his mother's, Carol Sanders, tragic accident. Sources tell us, he's been keeping incognito in Mobile, Alabama, visiting his dying grandfather, hotel magnate, Hank Sanders, who passed away three days ago."

A picture of a younger, healthier Hank appeared on screen before transitioning to an image of the Sanders Hotel.

"In an interesting twist of events, our source reveals that Dillon was the hit-and-run driver involved in Carol Sanders' accident that left her incapacitated."

The screen switched to footage of reporters hounding Parker outside Sanders Hotel.

"When questioned for more details," the reporter's voiceover said, "the eldest Sanders brother simply responded, 'No comment.'"

"Another interesting tidbit is Dillon's frequent visits to his sister-in-law, Natalie's younger sister who's been in a coma for nearly a month since a much covered-up accident at Natalie and Parker Sanders' wedding. Is there a connection? It's been reported that he reads to her. Apparently this prodigal son has been trying to do as many good deeds as he can to atone for his past mistakes. Only time will tell if his family and America will forgive him."

Natalie hit the mute button as she groaned. "Beth, no."

"Who's Beth?" To his own ears, his voice sounded small, detached.

"A friend, I thought. A co-worker."

"Co-worker?" Anger shot through his veins, ending his stupor. "Like a journalist? How could you be so—"

"I know, alright!" Natalie shot to her feet, tapping her fingers against her legs in a frantic motion. "I made a mistake! It's not like you're Mr. Perfect."

Jan-di let out a gasp, causing both Natalie and Dillon to zero in on her. She let out a choked laugh. "Do you think my water breaking is a good excuse to break the tension?"

Roses are teaching that the beauty of life will bloom,
once you have
taught yourself the lessons given by living with the thorns.
Grigoris Deoudis

CHAPTER TWENTY ONE

Dillon

"Dillon, where's a watering can?" Daisy peered up at him from under the brim of her mom's sun hat. Way too big, it kept flopping down over her face, forcing her to keep shoving it back. She refused to take it off no matter how many times Mickey teased her about looking like she had no head

He paused in the act of putting the lawn mower away. The grass was all cut and even now. "I think I saw one in the house." She ran off to find it as he pushed the lawn mower into the shed and wiped the sweat off his forehead with a bandanna he kept in his back pocket. "Good job pruning those bushes, Mick."

Natalie had taken Jan-di's mini-van to drive them to the hospital a couple hours before, leaving Dillon to watch the kids. He did the only thing he could do when he was under stress—he decided to create something and roped the kids into helping him.

After Dillon carefully uprooted the four neglected rosebushes from the front yard, he had the kids use their little, red wagon to haul them around the house. He also rolled a half-broken bird bath to the backyard as well.

When Mickey asked what they were doing with all this junk, Dillon had replied, "Making a garden." At least the start of one.

Daisy came bounding out of the cottage like her over-sized hat was on fire. "Dillon!" she shrieked.

"What's—" She barreled into his stomach and clung to his waist. "—wrong?"

"It's the ogre," she said breathlessly. "He's trying to break down the door. I heard him yelling."

Dillon almost laughed, but then he saw Mickey's scared face. A muffled pounding could be heard from the cottage. All amusement vanished. "Wait here. I'll be back." He broke into a jog and skidded into the house right before the front door burst open.

A middle-aged man in rumpled clothes and a five o'clock shadow stumbled through the entryway. His jaw sagged, appearing just as shocked as Dillon felt.

"What are you doing in my house?" the man asked, his speech slightly slurred.

Judging by his words and hazel eyes, it wasn't hard to figure out who this stranger was. Dillon almost felt sick.

He walked forward cautiously. A muscle in his jaw twitched. "This isn't your house anymore, Mr. Griggs."

The man cursed and shoved him aside. "Course it is!" He walked with a slight sway into the living area.

Dillon balled his hands into fists to force himself not to throw the man out on his face. He'd hurt so many people. Destroyed so many lives.

His hands loosened. He could say the same about himself.

"Hope!" Mr. Griggs' yell nearly caused Dillon to jump out of his skin. "Where are you, girl?"

When the man headed for Hope's room, Dillon shoved himself into the doorway to block his way. "You can't go in there," he growled. The vehemence in his voice caught them both off guard.

Hope's father staggered backwards, staring at Dillon with wide eyes, and for a moment, he appeared stone-cold sober. "You're right. I forgot. She's gone." He sank into one of the kitchen chairs and covered his face with a deep-seated groan. "She's dead."

Though startled at his words, Dillon relaxed his stance, still keeping a wary eye on him. "What do you mean?"

"She's gone," he moaned. "I killed her. I didn't mean to, but I killed her."

It felt like a fist to his stomach. His and Natalie's suspicions had been correct.

And he thought she was dead. Maybe it was better that way.

The longer Dillon watched Hope and Natalie's father sobbing, the more he saw himself, hunched over suffering because of the wrongs he'd committed. Wanting to wither away to nothing.

One word whispered through his mind. *Mercy.*

Dillon let out a hard breath, hands bracketed on his hips. "She's alive."

Mr. Griggs' shaking shoulders began to still. He looked up, his eyes rimmed in red. "What?"

"Hope didn't die. She's only in a coma."

"Th-that's right, I heard that…on the news. I forgot." A light began to dawn in his eyes. "I-I didn't kill her?"

Dillon wanted to say *You practically did*, but he just nodded.

Mr. Griggs surged to his feet and grabbed him by the shoulders, a wide grin on his face. "Then where is she? Where's my daughter?"

"No," he spat out. "You can't see her."

The man's grip tightened, smile slipping. "What do you mean?"

Dillon shoved his arms away and stepped back. "I mean, you aren't allowed to see her."

Anger darkened the other man's expression. "Who are you to tell me whether or not I can see my own daughter?" His volume escalated with each word he spoke until it sounded like a roar. "Who do you think you are? I—wait, you're that Sanders boy, aren't you?" Narrowing his eyes, he swayed slightly to the left. "Your brother stole my Natalie. You leave Hope alone, you hear me?" His voice shook.

"You need some coffee." And a therapist. "You aren't thinking clearly."

"You can't have her!"

Before Dillon could respond, Daisy let out a high-pitched scream in the backyard. He jolted toward the door and pointed at Mr. Griggs. "Stay here. I'll be back."

Sprinting out of the house, he found a red-faced Daisy trying to wrestle her brother to the ground. "What's going on here? What's wrong?"

Mickey shoved her off, but she grabbed his shirt. "No, don't!" She gave Dillon a wet, imploring look. "He said he was going to help you fight the ogre."

Running agitated hands through his hair, he glanced at the house. "He's not an ogre. He's just—" Releasing a low growl, he pointed at them in a commanding gesture. "Just stay here." He turned and strode back towards the house.

"Dillon!" Daisy called out.

"I'll be okay, I promise," he shouted over his shoulder as he broke into a jog. A sinking feeling began in his stomach. He shouldn't have left Mr. Griggs alone.

Entering the kitchen, he stopped stock-still before breaking into a run to the front of the house, back to Hope's room, then returning to the kitchen.

Letting out a frustrated yell, Dillon slammed his palms against the countertop.

The cottage was empty. Hope's father was gone.

Yanking out his cell phone, he started to call the police before dialing a different number.

Parker answered on the second ring. "Hello?"

"It's Dillon." He drew in a deep breath. "I need your help."

Hope

Well, they sure weren't rocks or trees.

I peered into the forest of giant thorns. They were reminiscent of the ones magically cursed to guard Sleeping Beauty's castle. Didn't at least a hundred princes die before one got to the princess?

"Um," my voice caught. "We have to go in there?"

Gardener took Dickinson's basket from my trembling hand. "No way around or over. Only through." He gently hooked my arm through his like we were going on a leisurely stroll.

I didn't protest or pull away or run. Not this time. And I believe that step in the right direction infused me with a bit more strength. However, when we entered the dark, thorny forest, I tried in vain to think of some distraction to keep my courage from ebbing.

My gaze swooped across the vines, and discovered thorns weren't the only things growing in this forest. Red roses peppered the area with much needed color.

"They're so pretty." I reached forward to touch one.

Gardener placed his hand on my arm. "Don't."

I snatched my hand back. "Oh. I'm sorry. I didn't kn—"

"No, look," he interrupted. He tugged one of the roses free. Wicked-looking thorns covered the entire stem.

I sucked in my breath when he began tearing the thorns away in quick, decisive movements. "What…" My question faded when he held the rose out to me, free of thorns. "Y-you didn't have to do that." Why would he do that?

"I wanted to," he said simply.

I received the rose, my gaze focused on his scratched and blood-ied hands.

The simple gesture overwhelmed me. No regular person would do what he just did. It was an act of someone who truly cared. It was something a hero would do for a heroine. A father would do for his daughter.

I twirled the rose between my fingers. "I don't know what to say except…thank you."

He smiled, his eyes crinkling at the corners. "That's plenty."

A small bud of warmth began to unfurl inside my chest. I tucked the rose in the sash of my dress, and we continued on.

'Hope' is the thing with feathers —
That perches in the soul —
And sings the tune without the words —
And never stops — at all —
—Emily Dickinson

CHAPTER TWENTY TWO

Dillon

The door to Hope's room at the nursing home closed behind him with a soft snick. Leaning against it heavily, Dillon rubbed his hands across his face and released a groan.

After getting off the phone with Parker and calling Natalie, he'd piled the kids into Natalie's car and drove them straight to the nursing home. Ms. Fi promised to watch the kids while he stayed with Hope.

"I don't know if it was such a great idea for me to come here or not." Dropping his hands, he walked around the bed and fiddled with the window latch until it opened, and the room was flooded with new spring air. Gazing below at the parking lot, he spotted the few stray reporters he was able to avoid by coming in the back way. "But things are kind of crazy right now, and I had to tell you something before it was too late."

Pulling a chair close to Hope's bed and straddling it backwards, he folded his arms on top of the backrest. It reminded him of the first day he visited Grandad.

"To be completely honest, I don't know what's going to happen to us." He pointed back and forth between them as though she could see. "Me and you, we have a lot in common, but I believe you held onto one thing I rejected a long time ago. Hope."

A short laugh escaped him. "It's ironic, of course…and fitting."

He toyed with the edge of her hospital blanket. "One thing I do know that's going to happen is that we both have a choice to make. You helped me make mine, did you know that?"

Hope lay still. The only evidence of life flowing through her was the beep of the heart monitor and the steady rise and fall of her chest. Wavy hair cascaded over her shoulders, framing a pale, slender face and closed eyes.

He wished she'd open her eyes. The image of small Hope from the photograph and his dream swam across his vision, merging with the young woman before him.

Dillon choked out his next words. "I was so afraid of losing those I cared about the most that I ran, hoping to freeze time and pretend nothing ever happened. I was just going to be gone for a while, you know? Until I figured out how to handle everything." He let out a shaky breath. "But I got lost, and I kept running, forgetting the earth is round. Leading me straight back where I didn't want to be."

Folding his hands in front of his mouth as though he were in prayer, he squeezed his eyes shut tight for a moment. "But," he said, his voice stronger, "it's where I needed to be."

Looking back at her, an affectionate smile stole onto his face. "In the course of all this, you helped me look beyond myself and discover I can do what I've been terrified to do. And I believe I was brought here to tell you the same thing." He slipped his palm beneath her hand, wrapping his fingers around it and giving a gentle squeeze. "Come home."

The vibration of his phone startled him. A text from Parker.

I'M SENDING SECURITY TO GUARD HOPE'S ROOM UNTIL POLICE CATCH NAT'S DAD. IF YOU DON'T WANT TO BE SEEN, BETTER LEAVE NOW.

Dillon shoved the phone back into his pocket. His heart raced, but he didn't rush to leave. He'd made his choice. No more hiding.

Instead, he gave Hope the advice he tried to use himself. "Breathe." He pressed a soft kiss to the back of her hand. "Just breathe."

Hope

The deeper we traveled into the thorn forest, the roses grew scant until finally there were none at all. I kept reaching up and touching the one in my sash to assure myself some beauty was left in this dark place.

The thorn vines were everywhere, growing denser the further we walked. They created natural walls and a ceiling with only a few slivers of light peeping through like veins of gold in a cave wall. A few times I was surprised by some smaller vines snaking onto the path, reaching out to trip me.

After the fourth time I stumbled, I almost asked the dreaded question, "Are we there yet?" when Gardener grabbed my arm and said in a hushed voice, "Look!"

My breath caught when I spotted Dillon standing a distance away. Hands in his pockets, he was shuffling his feet as though reluctant to come closer, but his bright, clear gaze was trained on me with a look of expectancy.

"Go to him," Gardener whispered, giving me a gentle push.

I looked back at him uncertainly before doing as he suggested. Stopping a couple feet away from Dillon, I twisted my hands into my skirt. "We've been looking for you."

He ran a hand through his hair as though agitated. "I don't know if it was such a great idea for me to come here or not."

My gaze darted around at the menacing thorns, and I suppressed a shudder. "I was wondering…"

He kept going, "But things are kind of crazy right now, and I had to tell you something before it was too late."

Concern pulsed its way to the surface. "What do you mean? Are you okay?"

"To be completely honest, I don't know what's going to happen to us." He pointed back and forth between us, his voice earnest. "Me and you, we have a lot in common, but I believe you held onto one thing I rejected a long time ago." His face softened. "Hope."

My whole body flinched at the word, startling me. Taking a step back, I rubbed my arm absently, the bandages keeping me from feeling my own skin. "Dillon…"

He gave a short laugh. "It's ironic, of course…and fitting."

Out of the corner of my eye I thought I saw movement. Had the thorn walls shifted closer? I motioned with my head toward the direction I came from in a nervous gesture. "Now that we found each other, maybe we should head back to the garden."

Taking a step closer to me, all humor vanished from his eyes. "One thing I do know that's going to happen is that we both have a choice to make. You helped me make mine, did you know that?"

I was sure the ceiling had lowered a few inches, but his question distracted me. "How?"

Dillon's voice broke as he tried to form his next words. As he finally revealed the heart behind the hurt he'd built up like a wall. "I was so afraid of losing those I cared about the most that I ran, hoping to freeze time and pretend nothing ever happened. I was just going to be gone for a while, you know? Until I figured out how to handle everything."

He let out a shaky breath. I wanted to reach out and give him a reassuring touch, but he plunged on.

"But I got lost—"

I smiled. My Lost Boy.

"—and I kept running, forgetting the earth is round. Leading me straight back where I didn't want to be. But," he said with a brave confidence he hadn't used before, "it's where I needed to be."

Opening his eyes, a warm smile filled his face. For a moment, I stared at him in awe. This was the first time I'd seen an expression of genuine, true happiness on his face. The affection he exuded reminded me of Gardener. I remembered him telling me how Dillon didn't speak to him anymore. Maybe the old Dillon wouldn't, but I knew this one would.

Looking over my shoulder, I started to wave for Gardener to join us but stopped cold, my hand stiff in the air.

Gardener and Dickinson were nowhere to be seen. In their place, a tangle of thorns had grown over the path at a rapid rate, effectively trapping us in.

Swiveling around, I noticed the path behind Dillon was still clear. My relief was short-lived when I noticed the walls were indeed slowly creeping in on us.

"We have to get out of here!" I gasped, brushing past him. "Come on!"

He followed but didn't seem overly concerned. "In the course of all this, you helped me look beyond myself and discover I can do what I've been terrified to do."

Terrified was right. All the symptoms of my fear came rushing at me like a wave. Tremors shot through my arms and legs. My breath started coming in gasps.

"And I believe I was brought here to tell you the same thing."

Everything froze when he slipped his hand in mine, pulling me to a stop. Even the thorns halted their steady movement. I could only stare at him, heart caught in my throat.

It's like everything was holding its breath, waiting for his next declaration.

"Come home."

Dillon's words unleashed a storm of fury.

"No!" I screamed as the thorns descended with vengeance, slamming down around us like a living cage.

One vine wrapped around Dillon's waist, attempting to tug him away from me. Our arms stretched taut as we struggled to hold on to each other.

"No," I gasped again, sobs tearing my throat. "Don't leave me alone!"

Dillon struggled to draw closer, but the vine constricted tighter around his waist, and he stilled. His gaze held mine for a long moment, both anguished and hopeful. "Breathe," he whispered, before pressing a kiss on the back of my hand. "Just breathe."

The world faded and blurred in a myriad of colors and shapes. My eyelids fluttered rapidly, trying to distinguish the jumbled images spinning like a crazy kaleidoscope in front of me.

Amongst the thorns were rectangular lights and splotches of sterile whiteness. A window framing a pale blue sky.

The shadowed silhouette of a person.

Jerking my hand away with a gasp, my vision cleared.

The next thing I saw was Dillon yanked into the darkness, vines crowding the space where he disappeared. Falling to the ground, I huddled in a trembling mess inside a thorn cage.

I was alone again. In the end, I'd always be alone.

The thorns had stopped growing the minute Dillon had disappeared, leaving me in heavy silence except for my sobs. Somewhere in the middle of my tears, I pulled the crushed red rose from my sash, clutching it between my cold fingers. Pressing it against my cheek, its heady fragrance invaded my senses.

"Breathe," I repeated, my voice shaking. I drew in another lungful of air, the sweetness of the rose filling my being. "Just breathe."

For seconds, minutes, hours, I wasn't sure how long I sat that way, simply drawing in breath after slow breath. As my emotions settled, a whisper of a thought tickled my memory.

While I breathe, I hope.

In my cage, in my fear, in my loneliness, I stared at the bruised rose in my hand and heard a bird sing.

At first I thought I imagined the sound. When it grew louder, I jumped to my feet, not caring about the thorns that tore at my dress and hair. "I'm over here!" I cupped my hands around my mouth. "Gardener! Dickinson! Can you hear me?"

For a long moment, only silence.

A bright blue streak burst from the thorns and circled my head, chirping feverishly.

"Dickinson?" I gasped, letting out a breathless laugh. "You're flying!"

The bluebird landed on my outstretched finger, cocking its head at me.

"Where's Gardener?"

He let out a tweet before spreading his wings and darting back through the maze of thorns. A few moments of hand-wringing later, I heard a voice call out.

"Gardener!" I responded. "I'm over here."

"Keep talking," he said, voice muffled. "I'm coming."

When his face finally appeared, I couldn't help the thick tears from sliding down my face. I wanted to say "You found me" or "Thank you." But all I could do was stare in silence at his bloodied hands. He'd literally torn through the thorns to reach me. Nothing I could say was enough.

I just fell into his embrace, wrapping my arms tight around his waist.

He held me for a long time, his cheek pressed against my hair, my tears soaking the front of his shirt.

My shoulders shuddered then finally relaxed. "Oh, Gardener, I-I—" Everything within me struggled to say the words, "—Dillon's gone. I don't think we'll ever see him again."

"What do you mean?"

I explained what happened.

Gardener pulled back. "Do you trust me?"

"What?"

He took my chin in a firm yet gentle hand and looked me straight in the eye. "Do you trust me?"

I blinked as I let out a quivering breath. "Yes."

He searched my eyes, his expression compassionate. "Then you can tell me." Letting go of my chin, he took both of my hands between his. His blood soaked my bandages, but I didn't care. "Why don't you really believe you'll see Dillon again?"

Tears slowly rose again, clouding my vision. I felt my jaw begin to tremble.

I whispered, "Because…"

"Because, why?" he asked when I wouldn't go on.

My chest heaved. The tremors moved to my arms and legs.

Gardener's voice was almost…pleading. "Because, why?"

"I don't want to go back!" The words that had been stuck inside me tumbled out and landed between us. Letting out a low moan, my head bowed. "I don't—I don't want to remember."

Gardener reached out and cupped the side of my face in his work-roughened hand. "But you do, don't you? You've always remembered."

Tears slid down my cheeks and dripped off my chin. "Yes."

Dillon

The door to the hospital room opened. A man with balding, brown hair and wearing a security guard uniform stepped inside. His brow furrowed when he spotted Dillon holding Hope's hand. "Sir, this room is off limits except to those with special permission from family. Who are you?"

"I am family." He resolutely straightened his shoulders and looked the guard straight in the eye. It was time to take Grandad's advice and stop hiding. "I'm Dillon Sanders. Parker Sanders is my brother, and Jacob Sanders is my father."

Before the guard could respond, a small movement almost stopped Dillon's heart.

Hope pulled her hand from his grasp with a soft groan and shifted her shoulders slightly. Her eyelids fluttered before falling still again.

Breath hitching in his chest and gaze fused to her face, his mind barely registered the guard's next words.

"…have to verify—"

"Did you see that?" Dillon jumped up from the chair, gesturing at Hope wildly.

The guard frowned. "I'm going to have to ask you to calm down, sir."

"But did you see that?" he asked, stressing each word. Could he have imagined it?

Confusion and apprehension was written all over the man's face. "Yes. She groaned and moved a little, but everyone moves when they sleep—"

"Don't you even know who you're guarding? She's a coma patient!" Dillon laughed as he shoved shaking hands through his hair, over his face. "I have to tell her sister."

Yanking out his phone, he dialed Natalie's number, all the while glancing at Hope, willing her to move again.

She remained still and quiet. Even after Natalie arrived, telling him Jan-di had a girl. Even after multiple tests were run. Even after Cooper came and gave them the news that Hope had developed an infection.

"It's common in coma patients," he told them. "But Hope's came on pretty aggressively. To be honest, I've never seen one develop this fast. We'll keep an eye on her, but if her fever doesn't go down by tomorrow morning, I'd recommend moving her to the hospital."

"Thank you, Doctor," Natalie whispered.

Cooper gave them an encouraging nod before he left the room, but Dillon saw the expression in his eyes. Doubt.

Clenching his fists, Dillon drew in a deep breath and released a prayer.

Memories are keys not to the past, but to the future.
—Corrie Ten Boom

CHAPTER TWENTY THREE

Hope

It was Natalie's wedding day.

The day I would escape. Or try to. Again.

But this time, I was determined to stay free.

Straining silently, I stood on my desk as I stretched my arm out the window, blindly trying to find the final screw I had loosened earlier so I could remove the bar that blocked me inside. The screw cut into my fingers as it twisted, and I bit my lip to keep from whimpering.

The bar popped free. I caught it before it fell to the ground, pulling it into my room and storing it in the closet.

That done, I stood in the center of the room with my eyes closed, listening.

Low murmuring from the television floated through the closed door, but otherwise, nothing. Dad was probably asleep.

My hands shook like hummingbird wings as I stored high-heeled shoes in my large, canvas purse before climbing back onto the desk. The purse slid out the window first, landing with a soft plunk on the ground in front of the rosebushes.

I paused again to listen, heart hammering in my chest. But no sound of outrage came from the other side of the door.

Now it was my turn.

My eyes shut briefly. I couldn't believe I was running away from home. That it had come to this. Wasn't there a way for everything to be wiped clean, to start over happy?

Shaking my head, I let out a hard breath and squeezed through the thin opening, almost panicking when the waistband of my dress caught on a splinter. Then I was free.

I trembled even harder in the unseasonably cold air as I slung my purse over my shoulder. One glance at the kitchen window proved it to be empty, but I sprinted toward the oak tree all the same.

Stopping to catch my breath, I peered at the rooftop of our neighbors that lived behind us. If I could just sneak through their yard and make it to the road, I could walk the extra mile to the convenience store and use their phone to call for a cab.

I clutched the purse strap protectively. The money I'd hidden away should be enough to get me to the hotel where Natalie was getting married.

A tremor of a smile graced my lips as I found a gap between the fencing and pushed my way through. My sister was getting married. She'd found happiness in a new life. I only hoped she'd let me be a part of it.

A gasp stalled my breath when I popped out of the other side of the fence. Despite the darkness that had just fallen, a young boy and girl stood in the middle of their yard gaping at me.

"I'm sorry!" The words fell out of my mouth without me giving them any thought. Force of habit, I suppose. "I mean, I was just finding a shortcut to the road."

The little girl crept a few feet closer, her eyes wide and shining in the light of their back porch as I stuck to the shadows. "I like your dress."

I blinked in surprise. Out of all the things a person might say after someone invaded their yard at night, a compliment usually wasn't one of them. "Th-thank you." I smoothed my hands down the peach skirt of my mother's old prom dress that'd been hidden in the top shelf of my closet. I hoped it was suitable for the wedding.

"What are you really doing in our yard?" The young boy had narrowed his eyes and crossed his arms. "If you came to steal our TV, our mom's napping on the couch. Even though she's going to have a baby, she has a black belt in Tai Kwon Do."

Despite the need for urgency, a laugh threatened to escape my throat. I swallowed hard and gave him a bright smile instead. "No, I'm not going to steal anything. In fact…"

I struggled to find an excuse and my eyes fell on the little girl's shirt that spelled "Princess" across the front in sparkly letters and thought of my sister wedding the so-called "prince" of America. "In fact, I'm on my way to a royal ball. I'm running late, and I need a ride."

The little girl's eyes must have grown three sizes. "You're a real princess?"

"Of course she's not, Daisy—"

She quelled her brother with a stamp of her foot. "Mickey, she just said!" Turning back to me, she said eagerly, "My mommy can give you a ride."

"HOPE!" The sound of my name exploding across my backyard and across the fence caused all three of us to jump.

An unconscious whimper escaped my lips as I ducked behind a thin maple tree. As if it made any difference. "I, uh, thank you for the offer," I whispered. "But I don't want to disturb your mom."

Cursing and more yelling resounded in our ears. My hands resumed their shaking, and I balled them into my dress. Feet poised to run, I glanced at the kids. They needed to get somewhere safe. "You two better go inside. Now."

Daisy sidled a couple steps closer to her brother as he asked, "Who is that?"

"Someone not very nice." The sound of my dad stomping around our yard caused me to panic. I ran over to the kids and herded them back toward their house.

"Like an ogre?" the little girl asked, her voice small.

Despite the situation, a sliver of amusement punctured my fear. "Y-yes, an ogre who's very angry with me for escaping my tower. I'm trying to get to the ball where the guards can protect me."

I kept glancing over my shoulder until we reached their back door. "Okay, go in and lock the door behind you."

To my surprise, Mickey grabbed my hand and pulled me inside with them. "You can cut through the house and go out through the front."

I didn't protest as the two children pulled me on tiptoe through the kitchen and down the hall to the foyer. Thankfully, we didn't pass where they said their mom was sleeping.

Before he opened the front door, Mickey paused and turned to his sister. "Go be a lookout, Daisy, and make sure Mom isn't waking up."

She gave a quick nod and moved to run away before doing an about-face and throwing her arms around my waist in a fierce hug. "Have fun at the ball," she whispered before running back down the hall.

Tears pricked the back of my eyes as I watched her go.

The feel of something cool and hard being pressed into my hand caused me to turn back to the boy in front of me. He'd just given me a cell phone.

"My dad gave me this in case I ever have an emergency when I'm not with them," he explained, his expression serious. "If you need help, just call 911."

"Mickey, I can't take your phone." I was a bit overwhelmed how well this young boy read the situation.

He crossed his arms. "You can just borrow it and return it later." When I started to protest, he cut in, "If you don't take it, I'm going to yell to my mom right now that you're in our house."

I swallowed hard as my throat thickened. It was my turn to give a hug. "Thank you," I whispered before opening the door. Giving him one more trembling smile, I slipped outside into the cold, night air, alone.

~*~

The first time I set eyes on my sister after five years, she was standing in the middle of an ornate bridal suite in a glorious, white wedding dress.

Apparently she'd sent all her bridesmaids and attendants away, because she was standing in the middle of the room alone when I entered. Her large, brown eyes shone with unshed tears.

"You came." She came forward with arms outstretched but stopped short at touching me. "When the hotel called up your name, I couldn't believe it."

I desperately wanted to fall into her embrace, but suddenly, instead of just relief of escaping my prison, I found I also had questions. "Why didn't you come? Why didn't you come and see us? See me?"

Natalie's eyes widened with each question. "I did call. But Dad said you didn't wish for me to come. Y-you were angry with me for never visiting, and…"

Her words faded as the tears I'd kept in check finally cascaded down my cheeks and a sob escaped my lips. "Oh. Oh, Hope, I'm so sorry." She gathered me in her arms, smoothed my hair.

I fisted my hands into her gown. "I needed you, Nat. I needed you." My voice broke.

Natalie drew in a deep breath and seemed about to respond when the door to the suite opened and a woman said, "Five minutes, dear."

My sister pulled back and shook her head. "We need more time. Postpone it a bit longer."

"No." I scrubbed the tears away with the heel of my palm. She deserved to have her ceremony untarnished by what I had to tell her. "No, we can discuss this later. You should go."

Her forehead puckered as she frowned.

I held up my hand with a smile before she could protest. "I'm fine. Don't worry about me. I came all the way down here because I'm so happy for you, Nat. And I really, really want to see you get married."

Tucking a strand of hair behind my ear, she searched my face. "If you're sure…then will you at least stand up with me as my maid of honor?"

Heart thumping at the thought of standing in front of so many people, I grimaced. "Thanks for the offer, but—"

"But you still get stage fright?" Natalie quirked an eyebrow. "Like the ladybug incident of second grade?"

I nodded vigorously as we both laughed. A welcome relief to

the tears.

"Three minutes," the woman at the door called out.

"Okay, well," she kissed my forehead, "I'm not leaving this hotel until we've talked and you've met my husband, deal?"

"Deal."

It wasn't until after the beautiful, fairy tale wedding took place that I realized I'd made a mistake. Again. I should have told Natalie everything when I had the chance.

He came for me during Natalie and Parker's first dance.

I didn't realize he was there until I slipped away to the bridal suite to grab a camera one of the bridesmaids had left upstairs. I'd offered to get it, since the whole bridal party was getting ready to do a surprise flash dance number for the bride and groom.

Searching through the pile of purses lying on the floor, I nearly jumped out of my skin when he spoke.

"I was worried to death about you."

Whirling around, I tripped over the hem of my dress as I struggled to stand up. He was coming toward me with a wrinkled brow, the hotel door shutting behind him.

He came to a staggering stop when I finally straightened. His mouth opened and closed like a fish, his eyes glazing over. Obviously, he wasn't any close to sober.

"Alison."

The sound of my mother's name almost stopped my heart beating. My blood ran cold.

The dress. I was wearing Mom's dress.

"N-no, Dad." Slowly, I backed up as he came closer. "It's me. I-It's Hope."

"No!"

I flinched at his shout. Began to tremble when his shock melted into outrage.

A cry escaped my lips when his fingers dug into my arm, and he yanked me in front of the full-length mirror.

"Look at yourself," he commanded, voice rough and shaking. "Alison, you should be ashamed. So ashamed."

"D-dad—"

"You left me!" He shook me so hard, my head hurt. "You left your daughters. Look yourself in the eye and tell me you regret it. All of it!"

"No," I gasped. I didn't mean to say it aloud, but I just wanted him to stop.

He didn't understand. He took it the wrong way. He was beyond reason.

He slammed me into the mirror so many times. So many times.

Shattering glass.

It all became a blur after that.

I remember blindly waking up to see him stumbling over to

the wet bar, sobbing as he clumsily poured himself another drink. Then I saw my purse on the floor just a couple feet away from my head. Reaching for Mickey's phone inside, I dialed 911, my hand shaking as I punched in the digits.

"Wh-what are you doing?" My dad's slurred question sent panicked adrenaline surging through my body.

Needed to get away.

With strength I didn't know I had, I pushed myself to my feet, wincing as broken glass dug into my skin.

Before he could reach me again, I'd opened the door and practically fell into the hall.

The floor and walls seemed to sway as I stumbled into a run. Cursing and heavy footfalls only caused me to run faster.

Thank goodness, we were on the second floor. I only had to get down the main stairway. Surely someone would see I needed help and stop him. It could all just stop.

At the top of the staircase, I paused. The foyer and the people milling about below swam before my vision. I went to take the first step.

"Hope!" my dad called out.

The use of my name instead of my mother's startled me into looking back.

I stumbled.

Falling.

Jessica Laurie

Cold. Sharp. Hard.

Darkness.

The Garden.

May you live all the days of your life.
—Jonathan Swift

CHAPTER TWENTY FOUR

Gardener held me as I cried until the last of the salty tears dripped from my chin.

"It hurt." I fisted a hand over my heart as my voice lowered to a pain-laced whisper. "It really hurt."

"I know." His voice broke a little, and he pressed a kiss on the top of my head. "I know." His arms tightened protectively as he rocked me back and forth.

When I let out a shuddering sigh, he combed the hair back from my face. "You know what?"

I leaned my head into his shoulder. "What?"

"I can heal whatever hurts you."

Looking up, I caught his smile right before he loosened his grip. Rubbing the wetness from my cheeks, he pulled me forward. With one hard yank, he tore down the last remaining wall of thorns.

227

My breath caught in my throat.

We stood in a stone courtyard with a fountain similar to the one in the daisy grove. I clasped the key in my hand when I saw what stood on the other side of the fountain.

The gate.

Gardener didn't point it out however. Instead, he pulled me toward the fountain. Eyebrows raised, he held out his hands, his request obvious.

I placed my hands in his, palms lifted up, and watched silently as he unwrapped the bandages and let them fall to the ground before moving to do the same with my feet.

Dried blood and dirt still cracked around the edges of jagged wounds. Though some had closed, they were leaving ugly scars.

Swallowing another sob, I met Gardener's gaze. "You can heal this?"

His expression was serious. "Do you want me too?"

To my surprise, hesitation still stalled my answer. But then I knew why. If he healed me, everything would change.

Squaring my shoulders, I shoved the hesitation aside.

Everything had already changed.

"Yes, Gardener, I do."

One of his marvelous smiles broke over his face. With sure, steady movements, he stepped into the fountain, swiveling me around until my feet settled into the silky depths of the water.

He removed a cloth from his back pocket, carefully took my feet in his hands and wiped off the dirt and blood before massaging them carefully. When he finished, he lowered my feet, and they tingled as the cool water caressed them. He went through the same motions with the palms of my hands.

As he cleaned, he sang.

Like my first day in the garden, his voice drew me in, but this song had no words, just a melody running deep like the underground spring that, unseen, fed the trees and flowers that flourished in the garden.

My eyes popped open wide when my gaze fell on the ugly mass of thorns. Roses unfurled their blooms in response to Gardener's voice, transforming what was dark and foreboding into radiant color.

Joys, tears. Longing, purpose. Peace, hope. All intertwining in one wordless song that stole my breath and fed my soul.

I now truly understood the flowers that blossomed at the sound of his voice. For I was awakening too.

When Gardener fell silent, I slowly turned my hands over and studied the palms. I didn't even have to look at the bottoms of my feet. I just knew.

Clean, smooth skin. Not a blemish in sight.

Letting out a shaking breath, I laughed. When my gaze collided with Gardener's, I found him laughing too, eyes crinkling at the corners. A tangible energy vibrated the air, and I couldn't remain still any longer.

Surging to my feet, I kicked up a spray of sparkling water droplets.

Gardener grabbed my hands and spun me into a dance. A wild, carefree dance with the breeze swirling around us like a gypsy shawl, carrying the perfume of the roses. Dickinson flew around us in maddening circles, singing his heart out.

The dance carried us out of the fountain. Gardener twirled me in and out of his arms as we spun around the courtyard, our feet stomping the ground in crazy patterns like a father and his little daughter trying to waltz to a frantic African drumbeat. Small flowers popped out from between the cracks in the ground and wall.

We were both laughing so hard, we nearly doubled over when we finally stopped. As we caught our breath, he led me in a slower, graceful dance, and inclined his head toward the gate, his eyes exuding warmth and contentment. "Are you ready?"

I stopped dancing and wrapped my arms around him, pressing my cheek to his chest. He held me tight as I listened to the strong beat of his heart. The sound of life.

"Thank you," I whispered, my voice muffled against his shirt.

He kissed the top of my head in response before I pulled away and faced the arched doorway. It was now or never, and I didn't want to wait any longer.

Tugging the key free from the cord around my neck, I stuck it in the keyhole, turned it, but didn't open the door. Not yet.

"You've made your choice," Gardener said softly. "Whatever is on the other side of that door, you're ready."

Closing my eyes, I drew in a deep, sweet breath. The warmth and brightness of the garden, of this place, had seeped into me during my time here. I felt it growing, shining until I just knew my whole being was glowing with the life of it.

Looking up into Gardener's fathomless gaze, I also knew I wouldn't face what was on the other side of the wall alone. Pulling the key out of the lock, I placed it in Gardener's hand. He gave me a nod of understanding.

Facing the door, I wrapped my fingers around the knob. For a moment, I heard Dickinson's lilting birdsong calling to a friend.

Then a whisper.

Hope.

A smile touched my lips.

Turning the knob, I opened the door and stepped onto the path.

Light.

Natalie

"Hope." Natalie tasted the salt of her tears as they streamed down her face, but she didn't bother to wipe them away. "Hope, can you hear me, sweetheart?"

Her sister's face remained placid and still, causing her gut to wrench. She wrapped Hope's hand in both of her own and pressed it against her cheek.

Natalie had been at the hospital for six hours, ever since she received Dillon's excited phone call. The sun had set a little over two hours before and with its disappearance, any expectancy of Hope's awakening she'd felt on arrival rapidly began to vanish.

"Sometimes these things just happen with patients in a coma," Cooper had said earlier when he'd examined her. "But unfortunately that doesn't mean there's any change in their condition."

Natalie chewed on her lower lip as her gaze slipped over the bouquet of daisies sitting on the nightstand Dillon had bought at the nursing home gift shop.

It would have been easier if Dillon had never come.

The thought surprised her. No, she was glad he returned. It was necessary. But…if he hadn't come then maybe her dad wouldn't be hunting for her sister, Parker wouldn't be shutting her out and no one would have seen Hope move, giving unrealistic expectation that she'd wake up soon.

Natalie squeezed her eyes shut at the unfairness of her thoughts, causing a few more tears to fall. It didn't help a situation to worry about blame, guilt and shame. It only causes more heartache. She tried to remember that when she refrained from blasting Beth earlier on the phone for releasing that story about Dillon. Yet another relationship in her life that was damaged.

Even so, she still felt the unrelenting burden of the choice she must make. If their dad wasn't caught or if Hope didn't show any change, would it be fair to keep her locked away in a hospital room, trapped in her own body—neither truly in Heaven or on earth—any longer? What if she never woke up?

Parker, Jacob, Carol, Fiona, and even Dillon were there for her now, as true family, but Natalie knew it was still her choice. She was Hope's legal guardian. Her sister.

"God, what should I do?" she murmured against Hope's fingers, her chest tight as she gazed at her sister. "Please come back. You won't be alone anymore."

"And neither will you."

Natalie started at the appearance of her husband standing in the doorway. "Parker." Without a second thought, she jumped out of her chair and flew straight into his arms, knocking him backwards a few steps.

Letting out a low groan, he crushed her to him, burying his face in her hair. "I've missed you."

For several long moments, they stayed locked in their embrace, swaying slightly back and forth, before Natalie pulled away. She brushed the backs of her fingers against his unshaven face as she stared at him unbelievingly. "You're here."

A crooked smile tipped the corner of his mouth. "I'm here."

The next words that she'd been dying to tell him face to face finally fell out of her mouth. "I'm sorry."

He stroked the hair back from her eyes, leaning his forehead against hers. "I'm sorry, too."

"My dad—"

"Has been arrested."

Shock spiked through her body. "What?"

She must have looked like she was about to faint, because Parker led her by the arm back to the chair and forced her to sit down. He knelt beside her.

"Yes, Nat. He was taken into custody less than an hour ago." He rubbed the back of her knuckles with his thumb. "After Dillon called me earlier, I called in favors and had the whole city combed, looking for him. We found him in a bar downtown. I don't even know if he remembers his encounter with Dillon earlier."

Relief and regret sluiced through her in a dizzying cocktail. Relief that she didn't have to worry about her father anymore. Regret at the father he never was.

Her gaze flitted back to Hope. The constant prayer that hovered around her heart resurfaced. *God, what do I do now?*

Parker rubbed a soothing hand up and down her arm. "You need to rest." He pulled another chair right up next to hers, beckoning her to lean against his shoulder. "Come here."

Natalie gratefully melted into his arms, already feeling her eyelids weighing shut. Even though she and her husband had a lot to talk about and Hope's future weighed in the balance, she felt like she'd still just received the speediest answer to prayer ever.

Rest.

And she did. The next hours sleeping sitting up in the hospital chair were some of the best she'd had in months, maybe years.

Sunlight shone ruby red through her eyelids as she began to stir. Somehow during the night, she'd leaned forward to rest her arms and head on the bed, closer to her sister. Though her back felt slightly sore from her awkward sleeping position, a contented sigh left her lips when she felt Parker shift beside her.

A hand gently tugged her hair.

Letting out a soft grumble to her husband to indicate she wasn't quite awake yet, she turned her head away.

Another tug.

Natalie reached out to grasp his hand. She stilled. Slowly, the realization that the hand she was holding wasn't large and manly, but small and feminine wedged its way into her consciousness. With a gasp, she bolted upright, startling Parker out of his deep sleep.

"Wh-what's happening?" he asked.

She only had eyes for her sister. Her sister, whose eyes were open and staring at her with a slightly bewildered expression.

"You're awake." Natalie's voice was thick with emotion—shock, awe, elation, gratitude—as she held Hope's hand against her cheek. A smile lifted her lips when she felt fingers lightly curling around her own. She was vaguely aware of Parker squeezing her shoulder and reaching for the nurse's call button. "Do you—" Pausing to swipe a tear that had escaped, she let out a soft laugh.
"Do you remember anything, sweetheart?"

Hope's gaze wandered and seemed to be captured by the daisies sitting on the nightstand

Dillon

Two lights.

Pinpricks in the darkness growing steadily brighter.

As he waited, he was calm. No frantic heartbeat. No tremors.

Just arms spread open, ready to embrace whatever came.

The laughter came like a song. Bright soprano melody, deep bass harmony.

The two lights became clearer.

Hope twirled into being, dress and hair flying around her like the petals of a flower.

As she spun, her form oscillated between little girl and young woman, pure innocence and wisdom flickering in her gaze and movements.

A partner joined in, catching her by the hands.

They both were suffused with such delight and contentment, Dillon's chest physically ached as he watched them. His arms lowered slightly.

A tingle of awareness zipped up his spine when the dance partner turned his piercing gaze upon him. He knew. This man knew everything.

Hope and her dance partner opened the dance circle and offered their hands to him.

He looked from Hope back to the man. "She's going to be okay, isn't she?"

"More than okay." The surety in the man's voice knocked Dillon's worries aside as if they'd been a pile of feathers.

Lowering his arms, he reached out and grasped their hands.

A smile creased the man's face. "And, Dillon, so are you."

The darkness disappeared.

Someone shaking his shoulder woke him up.
"Dillon," Parker's hushed voice washed over him.
Opening his eyes, he found himself lying on a bench in the

Jessica Laurie

hallway of the nursing home, the wishing fountain bubbling somewhere near his head. Early morning sunlight slid through the window blinds, dust particles dancing in their beams.

He sat up with a start. "Hope?"

Fatigue lined Parker's face, but he smiled. "She's awake. The doctors are astounded at how well she's doing."

A long, pent-up breath flowed from his lungs. "Thank God." He leaned his arms on his legs and bowed his head, causing his hair to flop over his eyes. She'd be alright. It was a real and true miracle.

Parker settled next to him and copied his brother's position of propping his arms on his thighs. "So." He glanced out of the corner of his eye. "What are you going to do now?"

Flipping his hair back, Dillon pressed folded hands against his lips as though in prayer. "Something I should have done a long time ago."

"And what's that?"

He dropped his hands with a sigh and stood up. "The right thing."

"Sounds like a plan."

Dillon cracked a grin. His brother always did love a good plan. "Yup, I've got a plan."

Parker rose to his feet, stretching his neck side to side to work out the kinks. "Good." He slapped his brother on the back. "I'll drive."

The drive to the Sanders Hotel was longest of his life.

Thankfully, Parker remained silent, leaving Dillon room to sort through what he was going to say when he finally saw his parents face to face.

Dad, if there's any way you can forgive me...No, no. He should start with, I'm sorry, Mom, sorrier...sorrier wasn't even a word.

You have no idea how much I've wanted...

"We're here," Parker announced.

Dillon looked up, startled to see they were parked right in front of the hotel entrance. Reporters lined the sidewalks. "Who called the press?"

"They never left," Parker replied. He lifted one shoulder in a sheepish shrug. "Sorry I didn't warn you."

Stepping out of the vehicle, they were assaulted by questions and camera flashes. Security and policeman tried to keep them at bay as the brothers pushed through the crowd.

Tension started to squeeze Dillon's chest, but all the worries and rehearsed apologies fled, when he saw the man standing in the doorway just a few feet away. Only one word escaped his mouth. "Dad."

Jacob Sanders, businessman revered by billions of people all over the world—who had every right to reject his lying, broken, coward son—couldn't wait for him to come inside and swiftly covered the space between them, pulling him into a tight embrace. "Son," he said, his voice breaking.

Dillon pressed his face into his father's shoulder like he used to when he was a little boy. All the noise faded in that one embrace. He wasn't afraid anymore.

When his father finally led him into the foyer away from the reporters, his breath caught.

His mom was sitting in her wheelchair at the bottom of the stairs, waiting.

"When she knew I wanted to greet you at the front, she insisted on coming too." Jacob laughed, brushing away his tears. "You know how she is."

Eyes locked on his mother, Dillon approached, feeling like a little boy again. "Hi, Mom."

Though she couldn't move, Carol's gaze sparkled with tears

but gleamed with love. It was better than a hug.

Letting out a short sob, Dillon knelt beside her wheelchair and wrapped his arms around his mother.

He knew—at last—he'd come home.

If you look the right way, you can see that the whole world is a garden.
Frances Hodgson Burnett, *The Secret Garden*

EPILOGUE

Hope

"Are you sure you feel alright coming here?" Natalie asked.

Closing the door to Parker's car, I slid my hands into the back pockets of my jean shorts and gazed at the newly renovated Garden Cottage. "Wow. It looks so pretty." I met Natalie and Parker's worried stares.

"I'll be fine," I assured them.

And I would be. To be honest though, it did feel strange returning to the house that held so many mixed emotions and memories. Especially since we'd just returned from testifying against my dad.

He would be in jail for a while. Ironic, that he was the one to be locked up this time.

For some reason, I felt no joy over the prospect. I knew how it felt. To be locked up and hurting. I didn't wish it on anyone.

But relief also caused my entire being to relax. As we entered the cottage, I realized that for the first time in a long time I wasn't afraid to be inside my childhood home.

Mixed emotions indeed.

I drew in a steadying breath.

Natalie's arm immediately snaked around my shoulders. "Okay?"

Giving her a shaky smile, I nodded.

Late afternoon sunlight spilled through the windows, dousing the polished wood floors, clean kitchen counters, and freshly painted walls in a golden glow. "Who did all the work?"

"We brought in a couple people for plumbing issues and to fix the roof," Parker answered. "But most of the clean-up and work outside was done by my brother."

"Would you...like to see your room?" The deep concern on Natalie's face caused me to pause.

After so many years apart, I finally had my sister back. Impulsively, I threw my arms around her and hugged her tight. "I'm glad you're here."

She let out what sounded like a half-laugh, half-sob. "I should be saying that, you know."

Pulling back, I grinned. "I know." Adjusting my flowing, daisy-white top, I approached the open doorway of my bedroom and stopped short. "It-it looks the same."

"Well, yes," Natalie said. "Your bedroom didn't really need any repairs besides a hole in the ceiling and taking the bars off the window."

The bars *were* off the window, and the window was open, letting in the sound of birds calling to each other and the wind rustling leaves.

I walked toward the window slowly, taking in each little part of my old room. Though I lived with Natalie and Parker now, this place was still a part of me.

The glow-in-the-dark stars on the ceiling that had made the night more bearable, the old quilt with flower appliqués I'd had since first grade, the books upon books that had become my journals in which to pour my thoughts and prayers.

When my gaze fell outside the window, I froze. "What—" I

gasped, bracing my hands against my desk chair as I stared. "How—"

"Would you like to go outside and take a closer look?"

I turned to see Natalie and Parker grinning like two little kids. Without a word, I brushed past them, flung open the back door, and stumbled down the steps before coming to an abrupt halt.

It was a garden.

My garden.

This backyard garden even had a gazebo like I'd drawn in a picture years ago, but with one key difference. An oak tree grew out of the center of this one.

Admiring the violets, lilies, and hibiscus, I meandered down the dirt pathway leading to the gazebo steps. I smiled at a butterfly floating above a rose bush, and almost gasped when a bird swooped upward after washing in a broken stone birdbath that had been transformed into a small fountain.

But my favorite part was the ring of daisies planted around the circle of green grass edging the gazebo.

Picking one of them, I stuck it in my hair before mounting the steps and breathing in the familiar scent of honeysuckle that had always permeated my backyard. It was a strange feeling to have dream and reality meet.

The person who'd built the gazebo had cleverly left off a covering and allowed the oak's branches to create a natural roof. I was glad, since that meant I'd still be able to climb the tree like I loved to do when I was younger.

I drew in another deep breath and caught a whiff of paint. Circling the oak tree, I discovered a guy kneeling on the ground, painting the steps on the other side of the gazebo.

He looked up when I stopped.

"Oh, hi." I awkwardly twisted the hem of my shirt around my finger. "I didn't realize anyone was back here."

He stared at me for such a long time I almost thought he'd frozen that way. He had nice eyes. Clear as a fountain pool.

I shifted my feet. "I-uh-so are you one of the workers?"

Finally, he blinked and shook his head as though to dislodge something. "Oh, um, no, sorry. I didn't mean to stare…" He set the paintbrush down and stood up, untying the blue bandana that was wrapped around his head to wipe his hands. Dark hair fell over his forehead in a distinctive wave. "I'm—"

"Parker's brother," I realized. "Of course. You look a lot alike."

A grin seemed to tug at the corner of his mouth. "So I've been told."

Shyness crept up on me, and I turned to run my hand along the smooth railing. "Natalie said you came and read to me while I was…asleep."

"Uh, yeah, a little." He let out a short laugh. "And just talked some."

Curious, I looked up again. "Really? What about?"

Leaning his shoulder against a post, he ran a hand through his hair before crossing his arms. He seemed to be thinking of how to answer. "Life, mainly."

He rubbed the back of his neck. "I was working through some things," he continued. "You made a great listener."

A grin spread across my face. "Well, I'm glad I could help."

He laughed. "Me too."

"And thank you." I glanced down then back up. "It's one of nicest things anyone's ever done for me."

For a long moment, he studied me again, and I didn't break the gaze. A smile crept up his face, back-lighting the blue-gray eyes that seemed to be able to see straight to my soul.

"What?" I asked softly, a bit unnerved by the strange connection hovering between us.

He shook his head slightly, but his smile stayed in place. "Noth-

244

ing. It's just…" Shoving away from the post, he strode toward me, hand outstretched. "It's just nice to officially meet you. I'm Dillon."

"Dillon." The name sounded familiar, like I'd already known. Parker and Natalie had told me. Of course. That was it. I returned his smile and offered my name. "Hope."

When our hands met, I almost gasped, but stopped just in time.

What a strange reaction.

He wrapped his fingers around mine and pressed them gently before letting go.

A bit off-kilter, I shifted away and gestured toward the house, the garden, and the gazebo. "Parker told me you were the one who did most of this. It's absolutely beautiful."

"I'm glad you think so. You inspired it."

I blinked in surprise. "I did?"

Dillon braced his hands against the railing and gazed out over the yard. "The picture you drew of a garden fell out of one of your books. This yard looked so empty except for the oak tree, and then I saw your picture and knew what to do."

"Wow. I was thinking this was my secret garden when I walked out here, and now I find out it is."

He cocked his head at me. "Your secret garden?"

"Yeah." I came up beside him and leaned my hands against the railing, mirroring his pose. For some reason, I was comfortable telling him about a part of myself that I hadn't told anyone else. It felt right. "Whenever I feel afraid, restless, or lost, I always close my eyes and imagine a garden. It's my sanctuary where I pray. Then when I open my eyes and leave the garden, I'm refreshed and restored."

Closing my eyes, I smiled as the breeze touched my face. I could see it. The colors, the life, the warmth, the freedom. The knowledge that I'm never alone.

"Now you've brought the garden here." I opened my eyes, and

contentment rose from my spirit when I saw the flowers. "There are no words to express how happy I am."

Dillon swallowed hard, his Adam's apple jerking in his throat, and he pushed away from the railing. "You know, I've always liked creating things for people. Maybe I'll turn it into a career. I like doing things—" He hesitated, a flush rising up his neck. "—to make people happy."

I tilted my head to the side. "If this is any indication, you'll be very good at it."

He studied me intently as though testing my words. "You think so?"

My gaze flitted from the gazebo to Garden Cottage to the garden. I grinned. "Oh, yes."

Dillon laughed as though suddenly released from a burden he'd carried far too long. He reminded me of a little boy. "Hey, it's almost time for Cooper and Jan-di's barbecue. I'll have to tell Parker and my parents I finally have life goals." His lips drew up in a wry grin as he headed for the gazebo steps. Glancing over his shoulder, he held out his hand. "Are you coming?"

In answer, I stepped forward and slid my hand into his. "Of course."

Our gazes held, and for a moment, it was just us and the breeze—like the breath of God—wrapping around us, scented with the fragrance of flowers.

Then we headed out of the gazebo and into the garden.

Acknowledgements

Every book is a journey, and every journey needs good companions. While writing *Breathe* I've walked alongside many people who have given me patience, honesty, encouragement, and much needed direction.

Jesus, Gardener of my heart, I thank you every day for the stories and creativity You've given me that I love to share with others. I now thank You for this one and the ways You used it to bless me. I now pray it will be a blessing to others.

Momma and BessMorgan, thank you for putting up with me on my grouchy days of writing and celebrating with me on my euphoric days. Daddy, thank you for the love of reading you passed down to me. Love each of you bunches!

Pastor Mark and Ms. MaryAnn Wyatt, it is finished! Thank you for being excited enough to give me this opportunity to publish my first, full-length novel and for being flexible and supportive this past year-and-a-half. I appreciate it more than I can say.

To my classmates and friends in Ms. Carolyn's Creative Writing course (you know who you are!), all the feedback you gave me in the first drafts of this novel was invaluable. Thank you.

Elizabeth B., Emily L., and Meghan S., thank you so, so, so

much for reading and editing through my final draft in such a short period of time. Sending out your book is never easy, and I had self-doubts galore trying to bring me down. When I received each of your encouraging and helpful comments and edits, I was beyond encouraged. Love you, girls!

I wish I could name every single one of the people who have blessed and encouraged me on my journey.

Just know, I love you all.

May the God of hope fill you with all
joy and peace as you trust in him,
so that you may overflow with hope by the
power of the Holy Spirit.
Romans 15:13

www.ingramcontent.com/pod-product-compliance
Lightning Source LLC
Chambersburg PA
CBHW022157260626
47155CB00019B/3067